# Out With It

Aled Islwyn is a writer, editor and translator. He has written and published extensively in Welsh, in which his fiction has been characterised by an emphasis on emotional concerns underlain by a sharp, lyrical intensity. He won the Daniel Owen Memorial Prize at the National Eisteddfod in 1980 and again in 1985. His collection of short stories, *Unigolion, Unigeddau* won the Welsh Book of the Year. *Out With It* is his first collection of stories in English.

# Out With It

Aled Islwyn

PARTHIAN

Parthian
The Old Surgery
Napier Street
Cardigan
SA43 1ED

www.parthianbooks.co.uk

First published in 2008
© Aled Islwyn 2008
All Rights Reserved

ISBN 978-1-905762-08-8

Editor: Gwen Davies

Cover design by Lucy Llewellyn
Inner design & typesetting by books@lloydrobson.com
Printed and bound by Gomer Press, Llandysul, Wales

Published with the financial support of the Welsh
Books Council

British Library Cataloguing in Publication Data

A cataloguing record for this book is available from
the British Library

*In Memory*

*of my dear friend*

*Marjorie Evans*

# Muscles Came Easy

*Muscles came easy,* I said. *Looked like a bulldog at eight, size fourteen collar at thirteen and captain of the senior school rugby team at sixteen.*

He was impressed, I could tell. Shuffled his arse on those pussy-sized stools they have at the bar at Cuffs and offered to buy me a drink.

Now normally, I don't. Don't talk. Don't look 'em in the eye. Don't do nothing once I've fucked 'em in the darkroom. Them's the rules. Walk straight out of there. Maybe have a drink on my own, or talk to Serge behind the bar, as I did tonight. Then go back a little later to see if it's busy in there by then.

Guess this guy just happened to see me there at the bar. Well! Let's face it. You can't miss me.

French, apparently. From Lyon. A businessman on his way down to Tarragona. Married, I wouldn't be surprised. But no

1

ring. Not your usual Cuffs customer at all.

Asked me if he could see me tomorrow. How naïve can you get? Didn't disillusion the sad fart. Didn't seem right to, somehow. Said my day job at the gym kept me busy. Wanted to know the name of the gym. And I told him. Said he'd look it up next time he was in Barcelona.

*Yes, do that, mate*, I said. But, frankly, I wouldn't recognise him if he pole-vaulted onto this balcony right now.

Then – big mistake! – he grabbed me by my upper arm and tried to lean over to kiss me. Jesus, man! How gross can you get? But I still didn't have the heart to tell him to fuck off, or that Serge paid me to prance around in the darkroom with no shorts on. It's Serge's way on making sure the facilities get well-used if it's been quiet in there for a couple of nights. I start the ball rolling in there if they seem a bit on the shy side. Pick someone I'd normally go for and give him a blow job. Sometimes it develops into a free-for-all. Sometimes not. But they've got to feel they've had a good night out, these saddos. That's what they're there for... supposedly.

For the most part they've got to grope around in the dark for themselves and find their own bit of fun, but Serge reckons someone like me making himself available for a while helps get things going. And it's always the start of the week he calls me. By Thursday, apparently, they need no encouragement. Never get these club jobs on a weekend.

Wouldn't have touched that French guy with a bargepole in my own time. Just didn't have the heart to tell him the truth. Should have really. I'm just too soft. Always have been, see!

Got up and left him after the kissing fiasco. Went straight back in there and fucked two more. Condoms worn both times, of course. Part of the game ever since I've been at it. Surprised how many of the older ones still ask and check. Guess they remember a time when it wasn't the norm.

Seeing the traffic going backwards and forwards kept Serge happy, I could tell.

Then the last dumb trick I pulled must have had this thing for armpits. Licked me sore he did, the bastard. Not really my thing. But he was good at it, I'll give him that.

Glad of that shower though.

First thing I always do when I come in from these club jobs. Check Mike's asleep (and he always is) then get cleaned up. Check myself over. Thorough. All part of the routine. Important. Never fail.

And so's this brandy. Part of the routine, like. Just a small one. Few minutes to myself out here in the fresh air. Mull things over. How it all went and that. Well-toned body. Well-honed mind. All that shit they pumped into you at college. Well! When all's said and done, it's right, like, isn't it? When you really think it over. Has to be... for the life I lead.


I refused point blank. Told him straight. I'm not dressing up in cowboy boots and stetsons for nobody – and no amount of extra euros.

*O, si,* he said, *but line dancing is all the craze now!*

*That may be so,* I said back, but I told him straight... he's running a great little health studio there. Raul. Legit. The genuine McCoy. Not some poof's palace where a lot of poseurs prance around pretending to lift weights and keep fit.

I'm strictly a one-on-one guy. Personal Trainer is what I'm employed as and that's what I am. Press-ups. Rowing machine. Circuit training. All the stuff I know really works.

I work with clients individually. One-to-one. Assessments. Supervision. Even down to diets and lifestyle choices. A proper trainer.

OK, I do some aerobic stuff with the women clients, I grant you. But they just like to hear the word used often. Don't think half of them know what the hell aerobics means. And told him that's all the pampering to fashion he'll get from me.

*Oh Joel, you not mean it! You think it over, Joel... please... for Raul!*

Love the way Raul says my name. And he knows it. They're not used to it here – Joel – which is strange, I always find. Spain being a Catholic country and all. You'd think they'd know their Bible.

He makes it sound like Hywel. Reminds me of home. Our Geography teacher was called Hywel Gordon. Had a hell of a crush on him at one time. He'd been a very promising full back, but some injury had put paid to that. No sign of injury on him from what I could see. But there you go! Guess it was the bits of him I never did get to see which needed scrutinising the most.

Raul's been good to me these last four years. Him and his missus. Helped me with my Spanish when I first arrived. Fed me. Gave me a job. *I only want best people work with me in my fitness studio,* he'd say. *And I want you.*

They speak Catalan together. Raul and his wife. And their kid gets taught in it at school. Like they do with Welsh back home, I suppose.

Not me, of course.

My nanna could speak Welsh quite a bit. Chapel and that. But I couldn't sing a single hymn at her funeral. And felt a right nerd. If there's anything of value to lose, you can bet your life my mam'll be the first to do so.

*Couldn't be arsed with all that, really,* were her thoughts on Welsh.

Then one day she lost her purse on the bus. Huge kerfuffle in our house. A whole week's wages gone. No wonder my dad left. *I'd have been OK if it wasn't for her with the glass eye from Tonypandy confusing me with all that talk about her Cyril!* The only explanation anybody ever got from her on that little incident.

Poor cow has even managed to lose a breast. *You're one nipple short of a pair of tits, Mam!* I tease her rotten sometimes. She laughs.

*You've got to laugh in the face of adversity,* she says... except sometimes 'adversity' slips out as 'anniversary'. It's a miracle I'm as well-adjusted as I am.

And I bet Raul has me taking these bloody line dancing classes any day now. I can see it coming!

*Don't know why you won't get yourself a tidy job,* she said.

I knew as soon as I picked up the phone she was going to take a long time coming to the point.

*Come back home and be a teacher. Papers always say they're crying out for them round here. And there's you there with all them qualifications...*

*I already got a tidy job,* I said. Why I bother explaining every time, I don't know. She'd never heard of a Personal Training Instructor 'til I started calling myself one – as she'll happily tell anyone who's sad enough to listen.

Didn't take a blind bit of notice. She never does. High as a kite 'cos of something. I knew it when she first came on the line. I could always tell, even as a child. Her voice almost croaking with that hysterical shriek she puts on when she's dying to tell you something.

*Our Joanne's pregnant again.* At last she came out with it. In one great torrent. *The washing machine's on the blink.* And to cap it all, the real biggy was her final punch: *Oh, yes...! And Dan Llywellyn has cancer.*

Then silence.

I felt nothing, really.

Said I was sorry to hear that, like you do without thinking. But I couldn't honestly say I'd thought of him at all for several years.

She didn't know where it was. *Somewhere painful,* is all she'd heard. The talk of Talbot Green Tesco's last Saturday, apparently.

He had it coming, I suppose. But I couldn't tell Mam that. Wasn't glad. Wasn't sad. Felt nothing.

*Still don't know why you started calling him Dan Dracula.* She was chipping away on an old bone, hoping she'd catch me on the hop. *Always thought it was cruel of you, that, after all he'd done for you.*

*It's because of all he's done to me, Mam.* That's what I wanted to tell her. But didn't.

He's also the one who introduced me to weights. Saw my potential. *Dan Llywellyn is the one who saw our Joel's full potential.* That's what he'll always be credited with. Showed me the ropes. Gave me definition.

*You're everything you are today 'cos of that man,* she declared with conviction.

She was right, of course. And she meant it at face value. Wouldn't know what irony was. Not my mam. If she can't get it cheap on Ponty market, she doesn't want to know.

Her kitchen floor was completely flooded, apparently. Took three bucketfuls of mopping to clean it up. And today it rained there all day.

*You call me a Muscle Mary one more time and I'll fucking give you a good hiding,* I said.

*I haven't called you a Muscle Mary once yet,* he replied, playing child-like with my left bicep.

Well! To be fair he hadn't. Not during today's debacle.

*Pussy-boys are so predictable,* I said. *I always know what's coming next with you.*

*You're just a slave to your ego, Joel,* he retorted. *And that's a very subservient place to be for a man of your physical stature.*

On the bed, Mike rolled on his stomach as he spoke, and lowered his voice to that detached level which always places him beyond any further verbal bruising. It's a ploy he's mastered to perfection. The aim is to intimidate me and exonerate himself. It's a tactical illusion, of course, rather than a sign of true superiority. It's a part of our game. A futile duel fought in a darkened room, while our neighbours, all around us, bathe in a siesta of rest and serenity.

Maybe that's why we laughed. Lying there bickering in our Calvin Kleins on that vast double bed this afternoon. It was the only thing to do. Our last hope of not looking ridiculous, even to ourselves.

We've lived together long enough to be both comfortable and bored with each other in equal measure.

I slapped his arse and told him to go make a cup of tea. And that's when my mobile rang, just as he opened the door to the living-room and let the light in.

This guy's from Valencia, right. The one who rang. Owns a

7

club, it seems, and wants me down there next Tuesday night to work his back room. Personal recommendation from Serge, apparently.

I jumped off the bed and stood upright to talk.

Two things, I said. One: Valencia's too far, man. Must be four hundred kilometres, easily. Don't know how much that is in miles. Gave up converting long time ago. But then relented when he mentioned the fee. Said I'd think it over. Oh, yes! And the second thing, I said: *I'm strictly a top. Hope Serge made that clear. This boy's arse is an exit only. Period.*

Silence! Think the aggro in my voice had been too much for him. All I could hear was the amount of money on offer being repeated down the line. And the sound of water boiling in the kitchen where Mike was doing what he does best. Being English.

I've tried to talk to Mike. But I can't.

The news of Dan Llywellyn's imminent demise has followed me around for days. Ever since Mam told me. *And all the memories slogged me in the guts!*

That's the last line of this poem by a guy called Harri Webb. We did him at college – *You see, it wasn't all boys running around in muddy fields and pumping iron,* I told Mike earlier – and I really loved his stuff.

Mike's painting at the time. What I still call the small bedroom is now his studio. Looks more like a clinic if you ask me. I've never heard of anyone being creative and so tidy at the same time. Whilst the canvas is awash with colour, Mike remains immaculate. But that's Mike for you.

He was only half listening to me. I could tell. He then informs me that he's never heard of Harri Webb. *Another one of your trivial poets,* he insists. But inside I know that he takes it as a personal affront to his dignity as an English lecturer that I've managed once again to draw attention to a lapse in his supposedly superior education.

He was still at it when Mam rang in the early evening. Painting that is.

Things are worse than first thought, apparently. For old Dan. He's at home. But he's shrivelled to a nothing and his hair's all fallen out. Sick every other minute, it seems. All over the bus back from town. So she said.

*And what's his wife got to say on the situation?* I chipped in. *The usual fuck-all, no doubt.*

Mam tells me to wash my mouth out with soap and water, but I tell you, that woman should have had 'I see nothing, I hear nothing, I say nothing' tattooed across her forehead years ago. She must have know what was going on. Wasn't deaf, dumb and blind through ignorance, I'm almost sure. And I don't think it was fear either. Doubt if Dan Llywellyn ever touched her. It was just indifference. She'd sit there like a beached whale in front of the telly, stuffing chocolates in her mouth, oblivious to the tip around her. And all I ever did was mumble some banality as I passed her on the way to the bottom of their stairs. Dan upstairs before me, usually.

*You go on up, love,* she'd urge me. And up I'd go.

*Twp* she was, I reckon. Probably still sitting there right now, incarcerated by her cholesterol consumption and jellied in cellulite, flicking from channel to channel in order to shut out the outrages going on around her.

I reckon our Joanne will go the same way. Already showing early signs of abandonment, despite all this breeding she's intent on inflicting on the world. In fact, I'm convinced it's

9

part of it. All these brats of hers are only an excuse for doing less and less. That's the reality. She has no creative aspirations in her at all. Not for herself. Not for her kids. Never did.

*Leave her alone. She only wants to give me more grand-children,* pleads Mam on her behalf. *Since you clearly don't intend to give me any.*

Joanne and Dean already have three. That was my point, I said. Why the hell would they want more? Going by the evidence so far, the possibility that some hidden pearl of genius is hiding away in their shared gene pool is pretty remote.

They scream a lot. Mam spoils them. Dean disappears down the pub. And Joanne gets fatter by the day, only admitting when pushed that she doesn't really care what the hell they do with their lives... *so long as they're happy.* This is the happy heterosexual life we're all supposed to aspire to, as lived halfway up a Welsh mountain. I swear the sheep have more fun.

It's all over the *Observer* apparently. The latest Rhondda bombshell. Dan Llywellyn arrested amidst allegations of child abuse. They've torn his house apart. Even removed the telly and the video. So it's a real crisis as far as his missus is concerned.

I chuckled to myself, but felt nothing. Said even less.

*You used to spend hours down that gym with him.*

I let her do the talking and grunted in agreement.

*And round his house! Some weekends, you practically lived there.*

Her hysteria was muted for once. I knew there was so much else she wanted to ask, but never would. Some places are too raw for even my mam to venture. I simply coughed. (This cold

I've caught has made me croak incoherently when I speak, making my silence sound less guilty than it might otherwise have done.) Mam's voice cracked in unison.

The mirror by the phone was briefly my only comfort. I flexed my free arm. And smiled at myself in approval. For a moment I remember wishing Mike had been there with me. But he wasn't. It was just me and Mam... the mirror and the memories.


Got a worse drenching that night than I thought at the time. Must have. 'Cos I'm convinced that's where I caught this lot. OK! I know I said I definitely wouldn't do that job. But did in the end, didn't I?

Fancied the run. That's what clinched it, not the money. When you consider that it emerged he wasn't paying mileage for the petrol, it wasn't really that much. But I hadn't been for a seriously long run on the bike for months. So, Valencia, I thought, why not?

The evening went well. Tidy little bar. Changed into my cut-off shorts and leather harness and did a few tricks.

Hadn't even realised it was raining until I came out the back at 4am. If I'd had any sense, would have asked that guy for somewhere to stop over. But in my mind, I'd been looking forward to those empty roads along the Costas in the middle of the night. So wiped the seat, got on and revved my way out of there.

How was I to know the 'Med' was due to have its worse storm for five years that night?

Bloody exhausted by the time I got back here. Had to keep my speed right down, see. Made the journey longer, which meant I got even wetter. Thunder sounding off all around me. Lightning. Hailstones the size of golf balls. Could feel her sliding underneath me. Probably should have checked the pressure before setting out. But didn't. Could feel them tyres fighting the torrent for supremacy of the tarmac on certain corners.

Exhilarating at the time. But glad to get home, I can tell you. It was already light. The sun all bright in the sky as though nothing had happened. Mike still asleep, thank God. Squelched my way to the bathroom to strip out of my bike leathers.

Well! It's been a week and I'm hardly any better. Still coughing my guts up. Sneezing. But the shivering's gone. That was the only hopeful news I could give Raul when he called earlier. Wanted to give the man some glimmer of hope I might return to work before the end of the week.

*The things you do, not to do the line dancing,* he teased, accusing me of being a fraud.

Cheeky bugger! I leaned forward and pinched his nipple through his T-shirt.

*I'm as honest as my prick is long,* I said, choking as I coughed as I laughed.

He didn't flinch. Just laughed along. I'm sure he'd be a kinky little bastard given half a chance. He knows I'm gay, of course. Always has. But we've never really discussed it.

That's what made it rather embarrassing when the phone rang. Raul was still here in the lounge when they called. Over there across the table from me. He could tell I'd sobered up pretty quick after picking up the phone.

It was some bloody detective from the central police station at Pontypridd. Well! You don't expect it, do you? Not in Barcelona during siesta on a Sunday afternoon.

It's another world, you see. That's what I keep telling Mam.

*Nice for a week, love, but wouldn't want to live there,* she keeping replying.

She must have been the one to give them my number. Didn't think to ask him where he got it from. And looking back on it, he didn't really ask me anything either. Confirmed who I was. That I knew Dan Llywellyn. That I'd agree to see them when they came over. And that was it.

Must be serious, mind... coming all that way just to see me.

*This coming Wednesday?* asked Mike in disbelief when I told him. *They are in a hurry.*

*Guess they have to be if Dan is fading fast. They'll want to get their summons served before the death certificate is signed.*

Explained very little to Raul after I'd put the receiver down. He had the sense to down the whisky I'd poured him pretty sharpish. Said he hoped I'd be better soon.

So do I. It's no fun, this sickness lark!

I guess I should have. But I couldn't, could I? Don't ask me why. Just knew I wasn't going to before they rang that bell. And all that talk of 'substantial financial compensation' he kept dangling like a carrot in front of my eyes throughout our 'little chat' didn't make a difference either.

*This isn't a formal interview, Joel,* he said. *I'm not obliged to caution you and you're obviously not suspected of committing any criminal activity yourself. We just want a little chat.*

He didn't have a Valleys accent. Couldn't really tell where he was from, the young burly one who talked. Impressive thighs though. He was lean and well-muscled. Not in my league, like. But I knew he was a fit bastard and guessed he probably punched above his weight. Wore a pair of safari shorts, which looked great on him. And a kind of pink cotton shirt, which didn't.

Found the heat oppressive, he said. Never been to this part of Spain before. Investigating serious allegations made against Mr Daniel Llywellyn who ran the Junior Gym and Recreational Club down Bethel Street for many years.

Well, I knew why he was there! He could have saved his breath on that score.

*How is he?* I found myself asking.

*Poorly,* came the reply. God knows why, but somehow I'd expected more.

He already knew I was gay. He told me so when he first arrived.

*Yes and very happily so,* I fired back with confidence. Thought afterwards that I must have sounded defensive and regretted saying anything.

*So I see. Beautiful city. Lovely apartment. Must be a very nice lifestyle.*

*I like it.* I found myself agreeing like a sheep. He was setting me up for compliance and I wasn't having any of it.

He also knew I was now working at a health studio myself. *A bit different from your old haunts back in Wales,* he sneered.

Told him I'd taken time off work especially to see them. He said he was grateful. But inside I knew every word he spoke meant something else.

Should have dropped Dan Dracula right in it, I suppose. The stupid bastard. But just couldn't bring myself to do it, see.

Then he said he knew it was difficult to talk about such things.

His mate, meantime – the little short-arse git who hardly said a word – is still sitting in that armchair over by the door to the spare bedroom. Fascinated by art, it seems. Had a good look inside and his eyes devoured every painting we have hanging here in the lounge too.

It seems I can get back in touch with them anytime... or so the talkative one kept reminding me. No problem... day or night. When I'd thought it over. If I could remember any little incident when I'd felt uncomfortable... I shouldn't hesitate. *Any time. You just call me, Joel.* Like all the other lads had done... the ones who'd come forward and were now in line for *substantial financial compensation.*

Wants us to meet again before they go back. Tomorrow evening after the gym closes. For a drink.

I suggested the Zanzibar bar on *Las Ramblas*. His tourist attire should look at home there.

We shook hands as they left. And I looked him in the eye. For the first time. Didn't want him to think I was scared of doing that. But it's not something I've ever been good at. Looking people in the eye.

Still have his card here in my hand. Detective Sergeant Gavin Hughes BSc. Can't remember the name of the other one. He never left a card. But I told Mike how besotted he'd been with his paintings.

*You see the truth doesn't always come easily in this life, Joel.* That must be his mantra. It's his favourite sentence, most definitely. Heard it so many times this evening, it's spinning round my brain. Which would make him happy back in his little hotel bedroom if he knew.

That was obviously his intention – to plant the seeds that would get me to spill the beans. But the truth doesn't always come that easy in this life, does it?

15

Should have thrown the sentence back in his face... and added 'Gavin' at the end, like he kept adding 'Joel' to the end of everything he said to me. Like one big strapping full stop.

Still, he got more than he bargained for one way or another!

A strange evening really. Don't quite know what to make of it.

*Sorry! I just don't do guided tours of gay Barcelona,* I said.

*Oh, don't be like that, Joel!* he pleaded. A wry, old-fashioned smile lit his face.

I gave in in the end. We ended up in Cuffs. Introduced him to Serge.

Shouldn't have really. Gone round clubs drinking, I mean. I'm still taking the antibiotics for my chest infection. Don't finish them till Saturday.

Added to which, Mike went ballistic when he heard I'd shown him some of the night-life here. *He's a cop, for God's sake!*

He's so paranoid, that boy! It's unbelievable.

I know he's a cop, don't I?

*I've done my share of hanging around in gay bars,* Gavin assured me.

That was much earlier in the evening, when we're sitting outside the Zanzibar, watching the world walk by on *Las Ramblas*. It's a warm evening. (Aren't they all, out here?) We down a few drinks. Just me and Gavin. His fat-git partner made his excuses after downing two beers in a hurry. Then headed back to their hotel. Needed his beauty sleep, he said.

Slugs do, I thought.

So that left me and good old Gavin, who proceeded to assure me that he didn't intend to talk about Dan Llywellyn all evening. But then again... *the truth doesn't always come easy in this life...* and he knew what I must be going through... how I mustn't feel disloyal... how wishing to put the past behind me was natural... but how I never would until I had all this off my chest. Oh yes, he understood!

Which amused me, really. He was jolly about it all. One of the lads. Leaning over. Sharing a joke, where appropriate. His hand on my knee when occasion allowed. All textbook, 'You can trust me, I'm a policeman,' stuff. I knew his game and went along with it all.

Why shouldn't I let him ply me with drinks? Buy me a meal? As far as he was to know, my tongue might have started to loosen at any second. The one right word from him could have triggered an avalanche of juicy memories at any moment. My guard could be down. Floods of steamy recollections could be streaming from my lips at any second. Salacious anecdotes. Times and dates and sordid details. All the conclusive evidence that would put Dan Llywellyn away for many years.

I'm the big fish he wants to haul. Worked that one out after he rang to ask to see me. And he virtually admitted as much this evening. I was, after all, Dan Llywellyn's 'star boy'. Played for the county at almost everything. Boxed for Wales as a schoolboy. Very nearly made the British Olympic wrestling team. Got to represent Wales in some World Federation weight-lifting tournament in Budapest at the age of eighteen. More trophies than my mam could cope with. Which is why half of them ended up in Nanna's house.

So it's down to me.

*You're the man who can nail Dan Llywellyn,* he tells me.

*Seems to me the undertaker will do that soon enough,* I said back to him.

He laughs at that and slaps me on the back. Furious inside,

I reckon, 'cos he knows I'm making light of his mission. But he's enough of a professional to know he mustn't lose it. I would, after all, be the dream witness for him, if only I'd play ball. The ending of this dark chapter in the annals of Welsh crime lays in my hands. And maybe old Gavin needs this one for his CV to secure promotion or boost his self-confidence or his reputation amongst his colleagues or whatever else he feels is missing in his saddo life. He knows he mustn't blow it with me.

Daft sod! Does he really think I'm going to dish the dirt on Dan?

Seven-thirty! The traffic's buzzing. And the sun is up.

I'm not exactly suffering. But I can't get going either. This coffee is just about enough to revive my mouth. The rest of me can follow later, once I'm doing some warm-ups down the gym.

Raul will already be there. Cleaning. Setting everything up for the day. He works hard.

It must have been two o'clock when we left Cuffs. Early really, by Barcelona standards. The place was hardly getting going. But I told him I had work to go to in five hours' time and that he was also flying home today.

All in all, he must have been resigned to the fact that his tactics hadn't worked.

*Guess I can't break you tonight, Joel,* he joked half seriously over our last drink.

*You'll never break me, man. All these sad wannabees who made these allegations against Dan, don't know what they're talking about.*

*Talking about tears in some instances, Joel,* he comes straight back at me. *The tales some of those boys had to tell have left them emotionally scared for life.*

*You'll never find me crying, mate,* I proclaimed adamantly.

*Ah, Joel, the world is full of men like you who've lived to swallow bitter tears.*

Tears are totally feminine things, I tell him. They're void of any maleness. It's a clinically proven fact. No traces of testosterone have ever been found in a man's tears. Only feminine hormones.

He was stunned for a moment and didn't know whether to laugh or not.

*Oh! Men have the capacity to produce them,* I said, *but no means of instilling them with any masculine traits. It's a fact.*

When the taxi pulled up outside, he placed his hand on my knee once more, just as I was about to open the door. He half turned to face me full on and willing sincerity into his eyes with all the power he could muster, he said, *Remember, Joel, I'm on your side.*

I'm convinced the line about 'truth not always being easy' is about to get another airing and in a sublime moment of panic, I kissed him. A smacker on the lips.

Think I meant it as a joke. Can't really remember.

Well! Yes, I can. It was and it wasn't. A joke, that is. I was confused. And high. And horny. And he responded. Old Gavin. There, last night, in that taxi his lips went 'Open sesame' and his hand moved up my thigh.

The taxi driver just sat there not caring a damn. He's seen it all before. And besides, the meter was still running. Why would he mind?

Eventually, my tongue slid free and I got out without a word. Just stood there gob-smacked on the pavement as he's driven away. My hand clutching the card I'd felt him slip into my pocket. It's the second one he's given me. I now have a pair. Only on that second one he's written his personal e-mail address in Biro on the back.

It's here in my wallet, hidden away.

I've no idea how he got my e-mail address. My mam is off the hook this time. Telephones are an integral part of her communications system. It's a well-known fact. But an e-mail remains a mystery to her.

However he got it, there it was this evening. Waiting for me.

*Thanks for seeing me. I appreciated it and respect your position. But if you ever want to relieve yourself of anything, you know how to get hold of me. My investigations continue. It's a sad and sensitive business. Hope we get to meet again, especially if things get clearer in your mind. Regards, Gavin.*

I couldn't reply immediately. What a relief!

Mike has had several of his paintings accepted by some prestigious gallery. He needed the computer urgently. I was banished out here on the balcony. No! Correction. I banished myself.

Hate these days when I've been for a check-up. So fucking humiliating. And six months seem to come around so quickly. Condoms and care are all well and good. But I'm wise to stick to my routine.

Mike pointed out that I wouldn't need to go if I didn't play around. The darkroom work really bugs him. He suffers from selective memory. *We met in a bloody darkroom, Mike,* I said. *Remember?*

*You're thirty-three now,* was his response. *Time you grew up.*

Perhaps he doesn't want to remember. It was ten years ago. Not here, of course. Not Cuffs. Ibiza. Another club. A holiday. Our first shag. No condom. No cares.

And now, it's not even a memory.

He'll still want me to accompany him to the opening of his exhibition. He told me all about it as he broke the news. 'Launch party' it's called. More of a small reception, apparently. Just critics and friends. He told me the date and to be sure to keep it free.

I'm still good for wheeling out as the trophy boyfriend, it seems. And don't get me wrong, that's fine by me. So long as Mike doesn't forget at which bring-and-buy he picked me up.

Being told you're all clear should give you a high, I suppose. But curiously, it doesn't. There's relief. And then this empty feeling takes over inside, as you stop off in reception before leaving to make your next appointment in another six months' time.

Raul's missus made such a fuss of Mike last night it was almost embarrassing. Her wonderful meal was already enough of a contribution to the celebrations. She's generous to a fault and I can understand why Raul lives in awe of her every act of kindness. I have never in my life lived with anyone who oozes so much goodness with such grace and I understand that it can't always be easy.

*It's only two paintings,* Mike insisted repeatedly every time she mentioned his triumph.

*Still two more than Van Gogh ever sold in his lifetime,* I kept chipping in, playing the proud partner.

We'd taken the champagne, of course. Not cava, Raul noted, tossing the bottle in the air when we first got there and catching it again behind his back, much to Mike's relief.

Things are pretty tight on old Raul, I think. His overheads are high and with another *bambino* on the way he can't have much money to throw around.

As we sat down to eat in their tiny kitchen, Mike ceremoniously popped open the bottle. And the kid starts throwing his pasta across the room in excitement. The rest of us just laughed and made a toast of Mike's success and cleared off that first bottle without a care in the world.

Raul suggested a spot of line dancing to follow and I told him to bugger off.

I flexed my biceps to amuse the kid and he in turn tried to knock the muscles back into place with a plastic hammer which must have come with the set of plastic blocks I kept tripping over underfoot.

As the evening drew on, we all seemed bloated and bubbly and larger than life. And I really hated the moment when I knew I had to tell Raul I'd be away another week. It seems so soon after the week I lost when that bug laid me low.

Needless to say, I needn't have worried. His handshake was flamboyant in his sympathies. He knew. He cared. He caressed.

*Si, si! You must, you must,* he said. And with that he fetched the second bottle from the fridge, saying such sadness had to be drowned immediately.

*He indulges you something rotten,* was Mike's verdict on the way home last night. *You're like a great big toy he just can't get enough of.*

*You used to be like that towards me once,* I replied. *What happened?*

It's not good that it's back.

Mike made all the right noises last night after Joanne rang, it's true, but he's so buoyed by his new-found success, his words just sounded empty and devoid of any feeling.

Even Joanne's voice rang hollow as she tried to speak through the tears. A combination of the waterworks and the Welsh in her voice. Like a drunken sailor trying to sing a shanty aboard a sinking ship on a stormy sea. The meaning made no sense at all, but you could still taste the salt on your lips as the song slapped your face.

It will be two years since I was last at home. That's the trouble. I've started to forget.

She won't come over to see me. Our Joanne. I've asked her. But she won't. Says she doesn't like the food.

Bloody ridiculous excuse!

The truth is, she's never been anywhere much, our Joanne. No further than the prenatal clinic. And even then, our mam has had to go with her every time.

Not the next time, though! The thought struck me like a left hook. Not if it's back.

Knew immediately I had to do the same. Go back. Take charge.

I had no chance to even ask how Mam was. Dean has a go at me as soon as he picks up the receiver. It was late, apparently, and I'd woken up the kids. He's always hated my guts. Likes to think he's something special with his fists. And he'd love to take a pop at me one day, I know. But the sad wimp has never quite been able to pluck up the courage, 'cos he knows I've won prizes for it. So it's hands buried deep, whenever we meet. Pocket billiards and a mouthful of abuse.

I know I wind him up, which doesn't help, but he's such an easy match to light, I can't resist!

*What are you doing sleeping round Mam's house, any road?*
I said. *Can't you provide a house of your own for your family?*

*Very compassionate, Joel,* he retorts, except he can't really
do sarcasm. He has to scream it at me, thereby missing the
advantage of the higher moral ground which had subtly been
his for his taking if only he'd played his cards right.

*You boys fighting again? You'll be the death of me!*

Mam could be heard almost physically wrestling the receiver
from Dean's hand as she talked. Her voice was full of sniffing.
More tears. I sighed and start to feel depressed.

It seems that she hasn't had the test results yet. I tried to
interrupt the moist flow of pessimism by looking on the
bright side, but she was having none of it. Easier to wallow in
anticipation of the worse scenario than hanging on to hope,
it seems.

I was glad to get off the phone.


So much for 'The old town looks the same....' It doesn't.

They've knocked half of it down. And the other half's
boarded up.

*I'll be next,* said Mam. *Already feel as though I've been
knocked down by a bus. And I'll soon be boarded up. Eight nails
in the lid should do it nicely... with some lily of the valleys from
you and Joanne resting on top just to set it all off!*

She chokes me when she speaks like that.

*Don't go wasting your money on me now, mind,* she
continued. *So long as you keep it dignified, that's all I ask. I
don't want anything tacky. And make sure your father doesn't
put in an appearance at the last moment. Don't want him
ruining my big day. He ruined the last one I had in that chapel.*

*Mam, don't talk like that,* I said.

*Well, the bastard turned up, didn't he?* Her loud voice brings high camp comedy to the cancer ward. *And don't think I'm the only woman who's ever wished her husband had jilted her at the altar with the benefit of hindsight. The world is full of us.*

*And if you hadn't married him, I wouldn't be here now, would I? Have you thought of that?* I said.

She's only trying to be cheerful, she answered, expecting me to laugh along. But of course, I don't. I didn't. And I can't. Can't cry either. Won't allow myself. I never can. Ended up just sitting there, telling her not to be so daft.

Had a long chat with the doctor a little later.

He'd no office to take me to. We stood out in the corridor out of earshot, keeping our voices down and shifting sideways whenever anyone walked past. The staff use that corridor as a short cut to the car park when they go for their illicit fags. It sees a lot of traffic. Our whispers had to blend in furtively with a sea of uniforms, camouflaged by smiles and the slight whiff of smoke.

She's been slightly overly pessimistic, apparently. That's what he told me. It turns out he's more worried by her mental state than by the cancer. Well, not more, maybe, but as much.

*You're going to be OK,* I tried to reassure her when I finally returned to the ward to sit with her a little while longer.

The doctor had just told me her depression manifested itself in laughter, so my heart sank as she roared hysterically in response. She lunged at me sitting in my chair, before throwing her arms around my neck and all but falling out of bed.

*It's back, my boy,* she howled. *It's back. And so are you.*

Listen to the darkness.

You can't, of course. That bloody clock won't let you. Like

it won't let me sleep. Five nights I've been back home and five nights I've just been lying here contemplating how much I hate that clock. I've always hated it. When it chimed away in Nanna's house, I hated it. And now I hate it here.

To put it in boxing terms, it seems to punch above its weight. Stands there in the corner. Looking petit. A wallflower with time on its hands. Delicate casing and a poofy face. Calls itself a grandmother clock. *The only thing of any value I ever got from my mother,* Mam says. It may be old, but I doubt it's worth much. Just a clock with attitude. A wedding present to my grandparents, in the days when even the cheap pressies outlived the marriage.

Hear that tick-tock measuring the emptiness; its tenacity audible above all the other anxieties throbbing in my brain. Like a bantam fighter, it just keeps coming at you. Wearing you down. Numbing your pain. Making you oblivious to the killer punch that's about to get you on the blind side.

Curiously, Mam asked about it tonight. The clock. She wants everything to be in full working order if she's allowed home tomorrow. Had I wound it up?

*No, but it's winding me up plenty!* I replied.

She laughed that exaggerated laugh the doctor seemed to find so worrying.

I've thought about it. That chat I had with him yesterday. She's not suppressing depression. More like celebrating her inherent over-optimism.

Mam will always laugh. She always has. It's what pulls her through.

I've made her bed up. Ready for tomorrow. Hoovered round a little. Even wound up that bloody clock for her. Well! It's what she wanted.

It hasn't happened, has it? Mam isn't home tonight, as planned. I'm still here on my own. Just me and the clock.

More tests are needed, apparently. They want to be absolutely certain. Of what, I'm not too sure. But it seems they can't decide what to do. The consultant has been consulted and the specialist has had his say. And the doubts that are mostly left unsaid are deafening.

I could tell she was down, bless her. And when I rang Mike earlier, he said I sounded down myself.

*I can feel the despondency in your voice,* he said. How profound is that?

*Well, is it any bloody wonder?* I bellowed back.

He always has to use big words to deal with any gut feeling anyone may ever have. It's his defence against any genuine raw emotion. Yes, I was pleased to hear the exhibition continues to be a great success… and no, he doesn't really care a damn about what I'm going through here. I could tell by his voice. He never has cared. That's the truth. Not about me, where I come from, or my family.

The trouble is, I don't really miss him. It's been ten days and I've only made contact with him twice. Both times, what I really needed to find out was how everyone was doing; Raul and the gang, etcetera. Things in the flat. Not Mike.

Dan Llywellyn turned up a lot tonight. Not in the flesh, of course – what's left of it! In conversation. A verbal resurrection from Mam.

I've know he's there, of course. Same hospital, different wards. He's in a lot worse state than her. She kept repeating that. Never mentioned dying, but I knew that's what she meant.

*He'd love to see you. Why don't you pop along and have a chat?*

She needn't have bothered naming the ward. I've known which one it is since I first went to visit Mam. It's where the terminally ill are kept. 'God's waiting room' the staff call it on the sly. It's out on a limb. The ground-floor ward nearest the gardens.

One of the cleaners I got talking to the other day told me it was to enable the earth's gravity to make their journey easier at the end. *Dust to dust, earth to earth, ashes to ashes...* she could quote the lot.

By the sound of her, she'd caught religion and I didn't have the heart to tell her it was probably more to do with the fact that they built the mortuary round the back.

I wound that clock in vain last night. And now I wish I hadn't. Really only did it for her. And she's not here.

A torture for my own insomnia. Should have left it to its own devices. Do unto time as time does unto all of us.

When I next see that cleaner, I'll tell her that. She looked easily impressed.

*It's alright for you, Joel,* he said. *You're one of the lucky ones. You got out. Looked after yourself. Made something of yourself.*

I told him to go to hell.

*I know you don't mean that,* he said, eyeballing me like a pneumatic drill as he spoke.

Then he went straight into this sob story about Darren Howley.

That was his name apparently; this gawping, chubby geek I'd noticed in Spar this afternoon. Looked around forty. A beer-bellied no-hoper. The valley's full of them. Except this one had a real talent for staring. I wasn't flattered. I wasn't angry. I just wanted Mam to recover quickly so I could catch the first plane back to Barcelona.

Well! It seems he was once a promising football player. Went to Dan Llywellyn for coaching. Ended up on drugs and off the rails.

*A life blighted,* Gavin called it.

It seems this Darren called him on his mobile after stalking me round Spar.

*I keep in touch with many of those boys,* Gavin explained. *Or at least I allow them to keep in touch with me. Feel protective towards them, you see. Seen so many lives destroyed.*

*Mine's not destroyed,* I started to protest.

*No, quite,* he interjects. *Like I said, you're one of the lucky ones.*

*Made things happen for myself,* I said. *No luck about it. Stuck at it in school. Went to college. Learnt Spanish. I'm a self-made man. Made things happen for myself.*

*The trouble is, the Darren Howleys of this world are wondering why the hell you didn't make things happen for them as well, Joel,* Gavin continues. *Or stopped things happening to them, is more to the point. Do you know what I mean?*

I knew by now that he was intent on saying his piece, so I stood there with my back to the wall and my hands deep in my tracky bottoms.

*They know you see. They know what you went through.* The verbal assault continued. I held my ground in silence. *And they can't for the life of them work out why you didn't put a stop to it. Back then, they didn't have your balls, Joel. They didn't have your brains. They were dependent on a bright lad like you to speak up and save them further misery. Speak up and break Dan Llywellyn's vicious circle. But you didn't, did you, Joel? Why is that, Joel?*

*I still don't know what you're talking about,* I said. *No one ever messed with me I didn't want to mess with me.*

*I know you, Joel. I just know.*

*You don't, mate! You don't know me at all...*

*And I'll get it all out of you too, one day – the hard way if I have to. But it will out. You listen to me good...* he paused a moment while a distraught-looking relative went scuttling passed in pursuit of a member of the medical staff. His half-turned eyes judged when she'd be out of earshot and, before continuing, his voice lowered an octave, just to be on the safe side. *One day, I'll have you there in front of me, just like you are now. Only it won't be a fuckin' hospital corridor. And you won't be looking so smug. You'll be crying your fuckin' eyes out, Joel. Just like all those other sad bastards I've met on this investigation. You'll be so relieved to have all that shit of years ago out of your system, you won't know whether they're tears of joy or anguish sobbing down your cheeks and nostrils. You'll just know that you've wrenched out a gutful of pus that's been there hiding inside you all those years, Joel. And I'll be the one you'll be grateful to for giving you the best feeling of relief you'll ever know in your life.*

*Dream on, sunshine,* I said. And he sort of smiled. Knowing it wasn't the place or the time to pursue it further.

The worried lady was making her way back from the smokers' den, the nurse she'd managed to collar barely hiding her annoyance at having her fag curtailed.

*Can't pretend it's not good to see you again,* he chips in casually as the two women made their way back towards the wards.

*Really? Gee, thanks!*

*How's your mother?*

*As if you cared!* I retorted sharply.

*Well, I sort of do, really, Joel,* he replied. He'd moved from menace mode to vague benevolence with barely a facial distortion, only the subtle shifting of the balance of his body weight conveying his new-found mood of conviviality. *How is she?*

If the mood had changed, the persistence hadn't.

*You're only here 'cos Darren what's-his-name's call reminded you that I'm still in town,* I said. Equally calm. Equally polite. I put a jokey lilt in my voice to neutralise the tension. *You knew I'd be up here at visiting time.*

*So how is she?*

*Coming out day after tomorrow,* I replied. It was like giving in, really. Telling him that which I'd only just heard myself from Mam. But what could I do?

*So you have tomorrow to yourself then?*

Found myself agreeing that I did, without thinking through any implications.

*Come play a game of squash with me tomorrow afternoon,* he says. *At my club. I'll sign you in.*

Played a little at college, but not really a game I ever got into. I'm built for bulk sports, not speed. Had to say yes though, didn't I?

The trouble is, these old routines of mine don't work here. This view's all wrong. This brandy doesn't even work the same. Not like it does when I unwind in the early hours at home in Barcelona.

Mam's lean-to isn't quite the same as our balcony. No warm night breeze. No sound of a city still throbbing somewhere in the distance. Just Welsh rain on the windows, so lacking in

31

force or purpose, you can see how it leaves the bird-shit untouched.

Beyond Mam's ramshackle excuse for a garden, I can glimpse the dawn creeping its way up the mountain. Typical of life here – all routine and no passion.

Except old Gavin's left me knackered tonight. So I guess the passion's always there, if you know where to look for it.

He thrashed me at squash, of course. No surprises there. I could barely remember the rules. Not that that mattered much. When you play with Gavin there are no rules, it seems.

Almost five when I got in. Coming out of his car, I could see some lights just going on in other houses. People getting up for work, I suppose. Routines.

As we drove back from Cardiff, I told him all that heavy stuff he tried the other day in the hospital wouldn't work with me.

He laughed with condescending candour and said, *No, I know,* as though none of it mattered after all.

God, his wife must be a tolerant woman, I told him.

He didn't say a word to that. Didn't even smile. Just drove.

*You never said nothing.*

The police had apparently told him of my reluctance to testify against him. And that was the most he had to say to me. Almost all he had to say to me. An anticlimax in the end. It was bound to be.

I knew it had to be today or never. Mam came home this afternoon. And no way am I going back to that place just to visit Dan Llywellyn... even a dying Dan Llywellyn.

*I don't know why you don't do the decent thing and go see him.* Mam's been nagging ever since I came home to see her. *After all he did for you....*

Sat her down in that foyer place. The concourse they call it. Large waste of space designed to delude you into thinking you're entering or leaving a grand hotel. Placed her bag by her side and told her I wouldn't be long.

The taxi was already late.

*The bus would have done me, of course,* she proceeds to tell anyone within earshot daft enough to listen. *But our Joel wouldn't have it. He's very good to me. Come all the way from Spain to look after me, he 'ave.*

I tell her to wait. Though God knows where I thought she was going to go without me.

*Such a sensitive boy. He loves poetry and all that stuff, you know. Won prizes for all sorts of things at school. Don't be fooled by all that brawn... he's a sensitive boy.*

Mercifully, her voice drifts to nothing as I disappear down the corridor. The relief I feel is short-lived, as I see Mrs Llywellyn coming towards me. On her way to sneak a fag, apparently. After years of chocolates and the telly, she's succumbed to the joy of a new source of brain death, it seems. A packet of twenty and a gaudy-looking lighter were clutched in her fat hand.

*Oh! What a good boy you are!* She oozed all over me. The sentence that followed the most she's ever said to me. *Your mam said you'd go to come see 'im before he goes. I know you'll do him no end of good. In there, sixth door along.*

All those visits to her house! Out the back with Dan. Upstairs with Dan. Picking up some piece of kit I'll left there. Dropping off some piece of sports equipment I'd borrowed to work on at home. He and me in our man's world. Her, silent and redundant.

She shuffled down the corridor towards the smokers' yard.

*Won't be here long,* are the first words I say to him. Could have kicked myself, of course. But take comfort in the fact that he never has had much sense of humour. ('Getting to be perfect is no laughing matter,' he'd say to me as a boy whenever I started messing around during any sort of training.) So the irony, like so much else, is lost.

He didn't really seem to be suffering. I felt a little cheated. But he's gone to nothing. That much is true. Just a sad shadow staring at me from the pillow.

*You didn't squeal.* He made his voice as loud as he could muster. *You never told 'em any of our little secrets.*

*It's a long time ago now, butt!* I said.

He struggled to move his right hand from where it lay on top of the bed, finally lunging for what he thought would be the safety of my forearm. When I pulled my arm away in rejection, it fell back on the blanket again without a murmur.

His face remained unmoved. No sign of disappointment touched those dark sunken eyes. He'd managed to sense my meaning without as much as a lilt of the head. All shows of remorse were held in reserve, ready for the big one.

*You moved far away, didn't you? Spain, is it? They told me you were far away... and wouldn't talk....*

Each little verbal outburst came shrouded in a silence with which he seemed ill at ease. Like memories of a life once fully lived. Once vibrant and clandestine. Now, dribbled onto pale pillows. Like small deaths.

They kept me there. Transfixed by curiosity. Those little words of nothing.

A gargle from his throat made me lower my gaze for a moment from his hollow eyes to his dead man's lips. The two thin lines quivered slightly, but remained perfectly dry. And I remembered the time he'd tried to kiss me. The only time.

I'd flinched in repulsion and lashed out with my fists.

Kisses were for girls and proper poofs, I'd thought.

Today, I know differently. My stomach muscles tightened, squirming at my adolescent reasoning. I drew in breath. The way I would before a lift.

There was no one there to see me. He has a room to himself. The dying do, it seems. It's a private affair.

When the taxi finally drops us off, it turns out Joanne's long since let herself in. What you call a surprise party, apparently.

The kids ran around like idiots and shouted, *Welcome home, Nanna!* when prompted.

To crown it all, when Dean arrived from work at the end of the afternoon, a dirty big cake appears. It's candles. And streamers. And most of all, it's a load of bollocks.

*She's in cancer remission, not joined the circus,* I shouted.

Mam didn't want that crap. I could tell.

But she's laughing as I went upstairs to change into my jogging suit.

Four hours later, it's her and me again. The remnants of a cake and a pile of dirty dishes in the kitchen.

She's gone to bed, exhausted. And I'm lying here in the bath.

It rained solid for the two hours I was out. And Gavin had his mobile phone switched off, it seems.

He caught me unawares. I'll give him that.

That first punch to my belly stopped me in my tracks. And I never saw the second coming, either. His fist colliding with my face with such clarity its terrifying thunder still throbs from the pit of my jaw to the top of my skull.

Floored in one fell sweep, he towered over me, asking repeatedly, *You were abused, weren't you?* His voice intense and calm. The emphasis placed on a different word with almost every repetition. It isn't a passion on his behalf; it's a technique put into practice.

In intent, my *Yes* was a defiant shout, but gasping as I was for breath, I know that the reality of my utterance was nothing more that a whisper in the autumn air.

Barely a mile down the hillside from the scene of my humiliation, Dan Llywellyn's remains were burning in the municipally-approved manner. Even as I lay there, stunned into neo-silence, I remember noting that I was thinking that thought.

Conspicuous contempt had been the motivation for our run. Or so I thought. His idea, of course. *Let's run while old Dan burns? I'll pick you up!*

Our fun run through the Pencwm woods high above the crematorium was planned to coincide with the very hour of his funeral. A show of disrespect. A symbol of indifference.

In reality, it was nothing of the sort, of course. It was his planned revenge. Now that it's too late for me to add a gold star to his CV. Now he's been humiliated by a high-profile investigation that's come to nothing. Now that promotion is that much more difficult to achieve.

*Yes*, I desperately tried to articulate a second time as I felt his trainers thundering into my ribs.

*And he buggered you? Go on! Say it! Tell me what I already know, you piece of shit.*

At that point, my hands tried to stabilise the floor. And failed.

I flinched as I saw his right foot raised again and aiming for my face this time.

Once again, *Yes* formed submissively in my brain. The trees above me swayed. The sky-blue faded. Pain was all around. Rolling over on the earth, my capacity for thought was consumed by it.

*Then why the fuck wouldn't you tell me?* This time, his voice doesn't come from far away. He's in my ear. I smell him close. Feel him grab me by my vest, dragging me to my feet.... *You stubborn Welsh bastard!*

Instinctively, I aimed a fist to ward him off. But one arm was already planted round his neck for balance and, staggering backwards, I dragged us both down. Drops of blood spraying both his face and the leaves beneath.

It's a long time later that I laughed. His outstretched arm ignored as I fumbled on the ground for a wrist-watch that somehow managed to get dislodged in the assault.

He only allowed himself a smile.

Finding the watch, I stagger to my feet of my own accord and follow him to the car. We're both mute.

My senses remain disconnected. Even now, hours later, the pervading pain is the only message any of them will carry to my brain with any conviction. All else is fluff. Pain stands alone. Still throbbing, black and sore. Thorough and unrelenting. Worse than anything my memories of a bruising youth can bring to mind.

Mirrors have always been my friends. Until tonight. The wardrobe door's been left unlock, allowing the reflective façade to swing away from the sight of me.

I can bear no light. I can bear no blanket. Tonight, I lick wounds. And curse.

*Just leave it there... and... and go away,* I said, straining to be civil to her.

If I've said I tripped and fell while out on my run then that is what she will accept as truth. That is what she'll tell the world. After all, that's what she told Mike. I know how Mam works.

*What exactly happened?* he asked in that tone of voice he reserves for cynicism.

*Oh! Mam exaggerated as usual,* I said when I eventually decided to ring him back. *You know what she's like. It's just a scratch.*

It was two days ago that he spoke to my mother. He just happened to ring almost as soon as I'd come into the house. Bad timing. I'd hardly had time to hobble to the bathroom to clean up before Mam could take a proper look when I heard the ringing.

Made the effort to take myself downstairs last night to ring him back. My mobile won't stretch as far as Spain. But I'm struggling for normality.

That's what you get when you hide yourself away in a darkened room. Self-absorption becomes self-destroying. Self-pity dulling you're ability to deal with the world.

The telephone rings. Not often. Just once or twice a day. Joanne. Some of Mam's cronnies. Mike. A social worker. The front door bell goes too. But that's an even rarer event. No symbolic roses have arrived to put my bruises in the shade. No perfumed bloom has been forthcoming to make tender my unsated nose.

A good bottle of brandy might have been the manly gesture. But, no. Nothing has been forthcoming from him. All I get are trays. Left on the landing by my mother as instructed. A knock on my bedroom door heralding each arrival. Mere supplies for a self-imposed prisoner.

*I'm OK. Honestly. Just leave me alone.* Had to shout at her several times before I heard her footsteps retracting that last time.

To all the world, I'm here to look after her. But the will to nurse anything except my own ego has left me. I just lay here on this bed, thinking that after this fiasco's over, I never want to come back to Wales again.

*OK! I'll go back for Mam's funeral,* I conceded. *But that's all.*

Mike just smiled over his cup of tea. I smiled back.

He doesn't believe me regarding almost anything I've told him since my return. But it's all true.

We were both up early this morning. Mike and I.

He had some faculty meeting at the university. Wanted to know if I'd met Gavin back in Wales. *You know, your gay detective friend,* he said, pretending not to remember his name. *The one who came here that time with his fat colleague with a taste for fine art.*

*Oh him!* I replied. *We collided once or twice in the corridor. But he never got what he wanted from me.*

Serge wouldn't believe me either at first, when I said I wouldn't work the darkroom for him any more. But wasn't too concerned.

*Don't worry. I find someone else.*

Maybe I wasn't that sensational after all. But maybe it's just that there are always others. Others who'll come do what we do after we're long since given up. Moved away. Moved on.

I figure darkrooms are like Wales. I won't go there again. Well! Only in my memories.

# Just Like My Jeff

'Of course he was alive and well when he left this house!'

For the first time since Stuart's arrival, Marc tried to instil some resentment into his voice. But to no avail. He still oozed his usual contemptuous self-confidence. He couldn't help it.

Stuart sighed audibly. He would prefer to spend an hour with a hardened criminal that a man like Marc. Not because Marc was clearly a very affluent and in some ways influential member of society. It wasn't even the façade of respectability which he perceived Marc as carrying, to shield himself from any need for moral evaluation. It was the man's inherent smugness which made him feel slightly nauseous.

Both men knew that it was only a slight twist of fate that had brought them together this day. The trouble was, neither yet knew where the twist lay. Or what its repercussions might be. Both exuded confidence and remained cautious of each other. They were two rational, intelligent men, forced to come face to face in an immaculately restored Georgian room, to contemplate the death of a young man whose life had been of no consequence to either of them.

'He wasn't depressed?'

'Not at all, as far as I could see,' Marc answered.

'Not even slightly melancholic?'

Marc noted the word. Was mockery its intent? Or was the other man genuinely flexing some verbal muscle to impress him? He could not be sure.

Either way, he felt the man was clutching at straws, and smirked. He knew what it was like to feign melancholia. He had seen the emotion mangled many times. Mostly in this very room. Many years had passed, it's true, but the memory of the one who had been prone to such poetic pretensions was never far from his mind. He never wanted it to be far from his mind. He never wanted the man to be far from his memory. Once painful, the past was now buried deep within himself and had transformed itself into a comfort – or so Marc liked to believe.

In truth, he was worldly-wise enough to know that such pretension always had to turn to farce before it could turn to tragedy.

'As I've said several times now, sergeant, he was fine when he left this house. I was half asleep and can barely remember anything about it...'

'Oh, come, come!' Stuart interrupted. 'You can surely do better than that. It's only two days since...'

'Dawn was barely breaking,' Marc insisted. 'Consciousness takes its time to register. At least it does now. For me. And besides, I'd had a few drinks the night before...'

'But not enough to stop you from driving?'

'The driving was much earlier. I've already gone through all this for you. Early evening, I went into town... I *drove* into town. All that is perfectly true. But the car was safely locked away in the garage by the time I started on the brandy.'

'But you had quite a bit to drink. You said so.'

'Hours later. When we came back here. That's when the drink came into play.'

'You need to consume a considerable amount of alcohol before you can bugger young boys, do you?' asked Stuart, sounding like a real policeman for the first time since he'd arrived. 'Or is it more a case of needing to make sure they are well-oiled?'

Marc's cheesy smile never faltered. He picked one of the cushions off the sofa and shook it with unnecessary force.

'He... what was his name, again? It was he who insisted on drinking as much as he did. First, one drink. Then, another...'

'And another! Yes, I get the picture. Pretty soon your best bottle of brandy is gone.'

'Oh, don't be absurd! You don't think I brought out the best brandy for him, do you? I can assure you that he never had a whiff of it. Sainsbury's best! That's what we drank. And very grateful he was.'

'And not only for the brandy, I suspect, sir.'

'What are you inferring?' Marc tried once more to sound indignant. And once more failed.

'I mean the general ambience in this beautiful room,' Stuart continued with confidence. 'I expect the lights were dimmed. One of your favourite CDs played in the background. You sat there on that elegant sofa discussing world events.'

As he mused, never letting the mocking tone of his words be reflected in his voice, he picked up a handful of CDs which lay there on the polished table. Glancing through them with a genuine curiosity, nothing took his fancy. He was unfamiliar with most of them and quickly put them down again, Marc's musical tastes dismissed.

'Very few of the details remain in my brain, alas,' sighed Marc. 'All I remember is the attractive twinkle in his eyes – that look I remember so well – and, well, to put it bluntly, the fact that he was available.'

As he said it, Marc sensed that, for the uninitiated, all talk of recreational sex made the phenomenon sound intrinsically uncivilised. For the mainstream straight world out there, it seemed that the socially-accepted rituals surrounding sex were necessary for the act to be palatable. They ennobled base passions and gave them a veneer of something more worthy. Marc was at a loss to understand the logic. The adrenalin generated was always the same, be it casual sex or making love or rape. It was the same with food. The belly churned away and the gastric juices spun into action regardless, be it feast, snack or forced feeding.

All needs had a clarity of purpose. The body wanted and the body got. Marc made no moral judgements. He simply understood.

What Marc didn't understand is why this lad got up so early and took himself to a wooded grove at the edge of town and hanged himself. He had no means of knowing. Perhaps he awoke hung over and could not face the day. Perhaps he was repulsed to find himself in bed with a man who looked so grotesquely old in his sight. Perhaps the snoring had been too much for him. Who the hell knew now?

'You must have spoken to him in the club?' Stuart suggested. 'When you picked him up?'

'Well, yes! That must be true. But all I can remember is that he looked cute as hell. Infectious laughter. Those eyes! That smile!'

'Did he bring any drugs with him? Poppers? Speed? Cocaine?'

'Certainly not. I would never have allowed such goings on in my house.'

'I have to get a complete picture, you see, sir?' Stuart explained. His own boredom with the truth of the situation was evident in his voice. 'Without the complete picture, I can't complete my report. Without a complete and satisfactory report, the investigation can't be closed. No closure, no peace. For either of us.'

'Once we came back here, he went into his shell, rather,' Marc continued to recall once more. 'It was as if he was almost nervous. I don't know why. He was clearly very experienced.'

'Nervous?'

'Before you get too excited, sergeant, I can assure you that everything which took place was consensual. Don't even think of taking your enquiries down that road. In fact, he was jolly affectionate. We sat over there on that grey sofa. And in between gulps of brandy he was virtually falling over himself to please me.'

'And in that I take it he succeeded? Pleasing you, that is?'

'Not at that time, exactly, no. I've never been one to respond well to a sudden and rather aimless bouts of fondling. Or having my larynx molested by an overeager foreign tongue.'

'How did he please you then? Later, I assume, when you abandoned the splendour of this room for the more utilitarian comforts of your bed?'

'To ask such a question is quite depraved,' Marc retorted. 'Not to mention the humiliation that's intended for me.' For the first time since the uniformed man first raised the heavy iron ring on the front door, Marc lost his rag. His face raged and his voice lost its affectation.

'None the less, I'm sure you'll agree with me that this little chat is less humiliating all round than having to testify in public, at the coroner's court?'

'A coroner's court? It surely won't come to that?'

'It surely will, I'm afraid. A sudden death. An apparent suicide. A seemingly healthy young man. And you were the last known person to see him alive.'

Marc blushed with embarrassment, but regained his composure. The confident smile rose again from the ashes of his sudden burst of anger. He had a meeting of the Chamber of Commerce to attend and really could not allow much more of his time to be taken with this matter.

'Was it one of these he used?' Stuart changed tack, picking up a glass from a display laid out on a silver tray.

'Ugh! Yes,' Marc replied.

'Denied the best brandy but allowed to drink from your best crystal.'

'Those glasses were the nearest to hand,' Marc explained. He was been driven to explanations, and he didn't like it.

Stuart liked the thought of being surrounded by the finer things of life, but as yet lacked the self-confidence to do so with impunity. He also lacked the means to afford them. A major stumbling block.

The house he shared with his girlfriend on an estate on the far side of town was a modest modern affair. Its content had convenience written all over it. Glasses had to be dishwasher-proof. The bedside table had to be small enough to enable him to set up his rowing machine in the bedroom. These were the practical priorities of a young life that had not yet found its true destiny.

The glass object which he'd caressed with such care was slowly put back on the tray.

'Did you know he was under psychiatric supervision?' he asked.

'No,' Marc replied sharply. 'Strangely, we didn't get around to discussing the mental state of either of us. Our minds were elsewhere, you see.'

'On a vast consumption of brandy, snogging and... and whatever you did upstairs?'

'Absolutely. Dead right.'

'Sodomy I take it? Upstairs? You look like the sort of successful middle-aged man who loves to take it from an energetic, virile young scallywag. Am I right? Or maybe it's the other way around? I'm never very good at judging these things.'

'You're terribly broad-minded, for a policeman. As a collective force, you're not meant to be very good at dealing with gays, are you? Not that I've ever had cause to complain. Rarely have much to do with you.'

'Respectable businessmen like you are not meant to have any cause for complaint,' Stuart replied. 'Defending the interests of people such as yourself is one of the main reasons for our existence.'

'My shops have been burgled once or twice over the years. Always a bloody nuisance. The police like flies around the place the following morning. Always very courteous. Sympathetic, even – well, some of them. No-nonsense in their approach. No one ever caught, of course. One shouldn't expect too much, I suppose.'

'It's not a matter of condemning you, sir. Or condoning you either. It's your indifference which miffs me, really.'

Marc decided he would refrain from touching anything in the room until this man had gone. He longed to pick up the picture of Jeff which adorned the piano, but told himself not to do so.

He realised that this was something he did often, almost without thinking. To touch, pick up and fondle were acts of restoration for him. It restored faith and old acquaintance and memories. It was a comfort, damn it. It was all his. He had a right. And now he resented Stuart's intrusion on that right.

On paper, the room was all his, of course. That was the legal position. The truth of the matter. But Marc always conceded that this large front room belonged to two people in reality. Jeff and himself. His money had made the room possible. Jeff's taste had made it what it was; a classic Georgian drawing-room in a classic Georgian town house.

Five years had passed, but Marc knew Jeff was still present in this room; not only in his silver-framed pictures, which littered every surface, but also in the fabrics and dried flowers. These were less overtly Jeff's, but in a tactile way, more potently captured his essence than any picture ever could.

'He was young, of course,' Marc conceded sadly. 'To insist on taking his own life in that way.'

'He destroyed himself! And for what?'

'Who did you say found him?'

'Some stranger. The usual story. A man taking his dog for a walk.'

'Yes, it's always a man taking a dog for a walk,' echoed Marc wistfully.

'A long history of mental illness it seems. Very unstable lad. Unpredictable. Had been from an early age.' Stuart drew on his research so far to fill Marc in on his most recent conquest. 'Grew up feeling rejected by all and sundry. Socially inadequate. Not very bright. Placed in care at the age of eight. In and out of children's homes.'

'And we all know what goes on in those!' Marc interjected crudely, only to be ignored.

'Wouldn't settle with any foster parents,' Stuart continued. 'Played truant from schools. Placed on probation for car theft...'

'A sure sign of a young man going nowhere fast,' Marc joked once more, before finally conceding defeat. 'You must forgive me! But you see, I fail to understand how any of this classic case of a disaffected youth has anything to do with me.'

'Within hours of leaving your bed, he took his own life, sir. Not difficult to imagine that the police would come knocking on your door.'

'No,' Marc conceded. 'Maybe not. He was clearly a very troubled young man. But I've now given you a very full account of my brief dealings with him. And, frankly, what happened between us was probably what happened to him two or three times every week. I refuse to feel responsible in any way.'

'You see, my problem is, sir, that I don't know how much of this you know already.'

'I only know what I know, officer. He was a smiler. An enchanting, naïve-looking charmer. And randy as hell between the sheets.'

'But it was the smile which first attracted you to him in the club? The old "smiles across a crowded bar" routine?'

49

'You may care to put it that way if it pleases you,' Marc responded, his eyes darting towards the nearest framed photograph of Jeff he could find in the room. How he wanted to touch it and embrace it! How hard he fought to resist!

'Sadly, smiles in noisy nightclubs rarely carry much truth,' Stuart concluded after a moment's thought.

'Oh, never!' Marc agreed. 'Especially not from a deprived and dysfunctional boy like him. I say that not to reflect badly on either his behaviour that night, or my own, but simply as a truth.'

'And randy as hell between the sheets, was he?'

'Sorry?'

'That's what you said. A moment ago.'

'Are you excited at the thought?'

'Not at all,' Stuart replied unflinchingly, standing his ground and staring at the other man with a chilling neutrality.

'I offered him breakfast, you know? We talked about it before going upstairs. Told him I was a dab-hand at making pancakes.'

'Was he impressed?'

'Yes, he seemed to be at the time.'

'His eyes lit up in anticipation of what might await him in the morning, when the night was through?'

'You could say that,' said Marc, once more mystified by the man's motivation for speaking as he did.

'But he didn't stay for them, did he? The pancakes. They remained untossed.'

'Indeed, they did. He must have forgotten. Or they clearly didn't seem such an attractive proposition by six in the morning.'

'Six in the morning, sir?'

'Yes, that's when he finally left.'

'How do you know that?'

'I woke up as he lifted the corner of the mattress. Looking for a lost sock, apparently. The light hurt my eyes.'

'You must have wondered what on earth was going on.'

'No, not really. I knew very well what was happening. He was leaving. And the bedside clock told me it was 6am.'

'You didn't ask him why?'

'At my age, sergeant, you don't ask anyone why they're leaving you. The possible answers are all too frightening to contemplate.'

Stuart allowed a wry smile to cross his face, finding a semblance of sincerity in Marc at last.

He wanted to conclude his report as quickly as possible now, sensing that he would never find a sustainable link of culpability between Marc and the deceased's death. All he could be certain of were loose strings hanging in the air. Never connecting. Decidedly untidy. But conspicuously without malice.

Touching upon sexual gratification, his girlfriend's face came to Stuart's mind. He was a constant lover. Sincere. Faithful. Forceful. Solid as a rock in all things. Utterly devoid of sentimentality. But loving to the nth degree.

'And you're quite certain it was six o'clock?' he re-affirmed without conviction. (Secretly, he was cross with himself for his momentary loss of concentration. His girlfriend was soon dismissed and his mind refocused.)

'Oh, one hundred per cent certain, yes,' Marc replied, failing to pick up on the other man's temporary discomfort.

'And you told me earlier that no money exchanged hands.'

'Absolutely not. No matter how much he reminded me of

Jeff, there was no way I'd have brought him home with me if he'd been rent.'

'Jeff?'

'My partner for fifteen years. He's there besides you.' Marc's head nodded towards the many photographs. 'I lost him five years ago, when I was fifty. Are you sure you won't take a drink? Some tea, perhaps?'

'No, no, I'm quite sure, thank you.' Stuart used the photo frames to travel around the room, from image to image. 'Did you tell him that he reminded you of your dead lover?'

'Oh! He did more than remind me of Jeff. He was just like him. An uncanny double. That was the only reason I noticed him in the first place. The only reason I invited him back. In himself, he was naturally of no interest to me at all.'

'Did you tell him so?'

'Yes, of course. He saw all these pictures. He could see it for himself.'

'And what was his response?'

'Nothing really,' said Marc. 'One of those coy smiles. That's all. That's the only response I wanted from him. Those perfect teeth and sparkling eyes. All so familiar to this room.' He sighed, a sentimental gesture of remembrance, before continuing, 'And then he let me make love to him one last time. I wasn't unkind to him, but the boy knew that's really all I wanted with him.' Then after a moment's pause, an afterthought occurred to him and he casually asked, 'You don't suppose that any of that could have had anything to do with his death... do you? Surely not!'

# Everyone Else's Lungs and Livers

I should have married Rod when I had the chance. Everyone said he was the perfect one for me and when we got engaged at university, I thought so too. But what do you know? I have to end up with Tom.

It turns out that saying this to my solicitor was not a good idea. He gave me what I can only describe as a 'look', sighed and rustled a few papers, suggesting that I focus on my current predicament, rather than dreaming of what might have been. Well! I know it's twenty years and more since I last set foot inside any educational establishment, but I think I'm at a sufficiently critical crossroads in my life to indulge in a little retrospection.

He doesn't like me. That's the trouble. But I'm stuck with him, I suppose. As I was with Tom.

Self-defence is my trump card, it seems. *Frankly, it's your only card, Mrs Jones!* he added wryly, more for effect than out of conviction. It's apparently regrettable that there are no records of me ever having to be rushed to casualty or having actually broken any bones, but lack of emergency hospital admissions and fractures apart, it seems my case is pretty strong.

Daisy has been a brick, I must say. Made an extensive statement to the police chronicling her father's litany of drunken outbursts. Or so I'm told. She has nothing to lose by telling the truth, I know, but yesterday I half feared she might tone it down just to spite me. Not so, thank God. She turned up trumps.

She waved at me while I stood in the dock. I smiled back and lifted my hand off my handbag. I didn't want to seem too gushing.

Rhiannon wasn't with her. Couldn't get time off work, it seems. But I got to see her for a few minutes after my little 'appearance'. Daisy, that is. Before they took me away. She hugged me, which seemed strangely dutiful and very un-Daisy.

Wish she was here right now for another hug. The trouble is, they're all lesbian in here and Daisy would probably feel more at home here than I do!

*We were most unlucky not to get bail,* he lamented.

What's all this 'we' I asked? He looked perplexed, this so-called 'legal representative' of mine. Whittaker, I think he said his name was. Or Whittal. One of those. He spoke as though he genuinely believed he was going to share my ordeal. But no doubt he's safely comatosed on his Slumberland at this very moment, whilst I'm the one in here trying to sleep amidst the noise and squalor.

They all know Tom, that's the trouble. Those tin gods JPs who sat there in solemn condescension. An open-and-shut case of the small-town bigwigs all closing ranks – even unto death... and beyond. A well-known syndrome. Especially here in Wales. When you're English and never quite fitted into the scheme of things, even after living here for a quarter of a century, it only takes a little matter of murder for the powers that be to show their true colours.

This fat lump I'm lumbered with for the night was quite impressed when I said I'd been charged with murder. Of course, I put the events of the last two days in context. Filled her in on all the juicy details of my married life. And she could see the bruises for herself. But I could still tell that I was a challenging contradiction to her normal clichéd expectations of life and that getting her head around this was going to take some doing.

*You don't expect a battered wife to use conditioner for her hair and have immaculate nails, do you?* she said with a mixture of admiration and disbelief.

*And by the same token, you don't expect a doctor to be a wife-beater, do you?* I replied. That shut her up. For all of five minutes.

I can't go home. That is to say, I've been let out. Bail was granted. That ghastly place is behind me. Forever, I hope.

Mr Whitfield couldn't help chirping, *There we are! I told you not to worry. I was confident we'd get it sorted this week.*

Those are more or less his parting words as I finally walk out through the front door of the Magistrates' Court and into a car, which is in marked contrast to last week's indignity via the back door and into a van. (I wouldn't be at all surprised if last week's fiasco was down to some incompetence on his behalf he hasn't got the nerve to own up to.)

So, I'm out. But not home. It's not allowed. The house is a 'scene of crime' now, apparently, and sealed off.

*I know it sounds terribly exciting to you, Mummy,* I told her earlier, when I rang to let them know where I am, *but everything from my knickers to my laptop are inextricably lost to me amidst this particular 'excitement'.*

*Your father and I never knew why you needed one of those modern fangled things in the first place,* she retorted.

Well, in fairness, nor do I now. It was to do with wanting to take an Open University course to begin with, I seem to recall. Tom's a good earner, if nothing else. (I'm still not certain where I stand with his pension.) And over the years, I've become accustomed to the extravagances many perpetrators of domestic violence apparently lavish on their victims after damage has been inflicted. That is to say, if they are not actually psychopathic, and never prone to the bouts of shame and guilt and self-disgust which made Tom seem such a pathetic wimp at times. Without realising it, I've actually grown to like that part of the bargain. I shall miss it.

A pale-looking police officer called earlier with some clothes. Half of them aren't the ones I listed, of course. That almost goes without saying. But there's the cheque book and some other bits and bobs I'd asked for. Not the laptop though. No doubt they'll be going through that with a fine tooth-comb, even as I speak, searching for any websites on the disposal of abusive husbands I may have accessed over the years. They're desperate for some evidence of intent, according to Mr Whitfield.

Murder needs intent, apparently. And all I've given them so far is desperation.

Just have to make the best of it, it seems. It's a condition of bail that I live with my daughter. So here I am, in this pokey little flat in Cardiff with Daisy... and Rhiannon.

*Daz and I are really glad you felt able to accept our invitation to come here 'til all this blows over,* she said as the three of us sat down to supper. Rhiannon, that is. To me, her booming, highly lyrical, sing-songy Welsh voice still sounds completely at odds with her solid frame. *I really think we ought to put the past behind us now. After all, we're all in this together.*

Well, excuse me! No, actually. We're not. We're far from being 'all in this together'. I'm the one who made the front page of the *Western Mail*. I'm the one who could go to jail. And how can I possibly take to someone who calls my daughter Daz?

Tom once said we should be grateful she didn't call her Omo. And we both laughed. So I suppose there must have been some happy times between us. It's just that they don't easily come to mind.

Mr Whitfield sighed audibly. I think I'm getting to him slowly.

The murder charge has been reduced to manslaughter. Well! Of course I'm pleased. But I couldn't help thinking that this was also rather disappointing. This 'thought' I speak out loud. And it doesn't go down well.

*They used to hang people for what you did, Mrs Jones,* he tells me.

*Oh I know!* I replied. *And in America they still use that ghastly electric chair contraption. But I live in Abertrisant and that sort of thing simply doesn't go on there.*

Everyone knows what you mean with murder. It's biblical and raw and easily understood across all cultures and times.

Manslaughter has an altogether more sophisticated air to it. It's a made-up word, to cover a load of legal technicalities and given credence by this age of euphemism of ours. It's messier and less emotive. Give me a good old-fashioned murder every time.

He turned slightly pink. And then hurriedly turned to details of tomorrow's funeral.

Getting rid of Tom was a savage, sudden, unforgivable act of exploding emotion. By contrast, disposing of him has proved to be a most tedious and didactic process. Delicate deliberations between the coroner, the police, Daisy and the paternal side of her family went on for days before anything resembling a date could be agreed upon. Surprisingly, even I, it seems, have rights in the matter. Hence, the wittering Mr Whitfield is 'looking after my interests' in the affair, as the saying goes. (You read of such cases in the paper and never think of little details such as who arranged the funeral, do you?)

Given my 'position' I shan't be going, of course. Tom's brother, Peter, has assumed the role of chief mourner. Alongside Daisy, that is. But naturally, she didn't want much to do with the tedious business of actually having to arrange things. After making sure strict limits had been placed on the amount of money to be taken from her father's estate, she left it all to the saintly Peter.

Daddy thought I had been provocative with Mr Whitfield when I told him and Mummy of my outburst in reaction to the news, *As usual!* he added. This is rich, coming from the man who insisted on driving all the way from Surrey to attend tomorrow's 'sad occasion'.

They never took to Tom from the start. My parents. Saw right through him, I think, despite his charm. They took comfort in the distance between us and never seemed too disappointed that Daisy and I nearly always went down to see them alone.

I've pleaded with them not to come. Ever since we've known tomorrow's ordeal was looming. They're frail and eighty and can't be far from being the centre-pieces of such occasions themselves. But Daddy's always had this obsession with 'doing the right thing'. *We ought to ensure that our side of the family is adequately represented,* he said again over dinner.

They insisted that I join them at the hotel tonight. I didn't want to go. Miserable meal. Miserable conversation. They were tired. I'm tetchy. And frankly, I'm glad to be back in my cosy little boxroom.

Manslaughter is an improvement on murder, I suppose. From the point of view of my future prospects. Just not as glamorous, that's all.

Yes, I too was surprised by the comparative lack of blood. Initially. As he staggered from appliance to appliance around the kitchen, very little seemed to flow. It's only as we're waiting for the ambulance and police to arrive that I notice the little red rivulet flowing from underneath his shirt across the kitchen floor. He'd actually slumped to the ground before I even rang 999, I explained. He's clutching his chest and his eyes are still open. There really was a profusion of blood in the end, I tell her. It just didn't gush forward like an eruption, as you see so often on television.

*They do exaggerate these things, don't they?* she comments.

*Yes, they do,* I find myself agreeing with an alacrity which even at the time seemed absurd.

59

My mother is such a stickler for detail. I daren't spare her a single detail.

Privately, I think she's glad of the relief. Not light relief, exactly. No. But a relief nonetheless. This conversation isn't just the result of curiosity – it's an escape. The lurid minutiae of that ghastly night a contrast to the dull, self-inflicted heartache they'd endured earlier at the funeral.

They were all shunned by Tom's family. Even Daisy. The three of them broke down crying as soon as they entered the flat.

Rhiannon's nursing skills came to the fore, advising rests and cups of tea all round, which the traumatised trio accepted without question, only surfacing again from their delegated beds and sofas when it was time for the local news at six.

*The people of the close-knit community of Abertrisant turned out in force today to pay their last respects to popular local GP, Dr Tom Jones. The normally sleepy little town is still coming to terms with his sudden and violent death two months ago. His widow, Belinda Jones, has been charged with manslaughter and is expected to stand trial in the Autumn.*

The five of us sat through the short footage with a seemingly equal measure of solemnity. Only Daisy started to cry again as soon as they moved on to the talented pets convention being held in Builth Wells.

I took a pride in seeing her walk behind the coffin with her uncle, but left the job of offering her some comfort to Rhiannon. That seemed the most appropriate course of action.

Her grandparents looked the other way in embarrassment at this point. I felt a part of the same embarrassment, but failed to look away. I envy her, her age and wisdom.

When we're all composed again, we're hungry. (Daddy chips in that the breakfast served in their hotel that morning was grossly overpriced for what you got. Mummy agrees and we all shake our heads in indignation at the scandal of hotel prices in Cardiff.) In the end, Rhiannon drove to fetch some take-away pizzas. None of us felt like cooking. And in the circumstances, going out to a restaurant somehow wouldn't have seemed right.

Today was the day I buried Tom. Except I've buried nothing. And felt very little.

Was I alright? Did I need help? Was my legal team sufficiently sympathetic? *Yes, yes, and sort of*, I replied. Adding that despite his shortcomings, I was beginning to enjoy seeing Mr Whitfield try to conceal his animosity towards me and was looking forward to tormenting him further over the coming months.

My plight, it seems, has come to the attention of one of these support groups for victims of domestic violence. All very worthy, of course. And since she rang two days ago, I've envisaged a team of them on a daily quest, scouring through every newspaper in the land, looking for suitable cases to champion.

Her name's Celena and I invite her to tea. This clearly doesn't go down well at first. But after a few nervous chuckles and an *Are you sure?* or two, she agrees.

Not wishing to bring her here – Daisy and Rhiannon have turned this flat into a shrine to girliedom; even the toilet roll is covered with a frilly, knitted cosy – I suggest the Red Dragon Resort Hotel down in the Bay. My rationale being that the severe decor will create the right backdrop to the serious issues we have to discuss. And I have to say, I think I was proved right.

Starting off by saying I feel sorry for Tom proves to be contentious right away. It's alright to say I'm sorry he's dead, it seems, but not to actually say I felt sorry for him, the man. Which in fact I do. I always did. In fact, I tell her that I would go so far as to say that I feel more sorry for him than I do sorrow.

*You're a feisty woman,* she compromises at last, more out of a curiosity to hear the rest of my story than any genuine capitulation of ground on the issue. My 'story' is, after all, what she wants. And I don't hold back. My career disappointment. My love of Tom. Tom's drunken rages. Tom's cunning application of his professional skills to hide my injuries from too much public scrutiny. Tom's tender side. Well! All in all, Tom tends to hog our conversation.

Not to mention Daisy. Our one and only. Which, after the briefest of respites, brings Tom back to the fore. His resentment of my inability to bear any more children. His unwillingness to accept her lesbianism. The sarcasm. The anger. The downright nastiness that used to spew forth. I spare her nothing. And although I say so myself, my instinct in this regard, is impeccable. From the very first mention of lesbianism, I have Celena practically eating out of my hand. An embarrassing unmentionable in Abertrisant is clearly all the rage in Cardiff.

*It's a shame you didn't come to us years ago,* she judged thoughtfully. *Our number is in the book and we have a website. There are so many agencies like ourselves who could have averted this tragedy and saved you and your daughter an awful lot of grief.*

*We coped, you see,* I retorted. *That's what people like Tom and I are expected to do.*

*Did you, though? I don't think so.* She came back strongly, unnerving me for a moment.

*The violence was always so occasional and arbitrary,* I shrugged. *It hardly seemed worth it.* Adding in haste, to cover my tracks, that each attack clearly left a residue of anger in the pit of my stomach.

*Exactly,* she proclaimed with enthusiasm. *Over the years, you had become a time bomb of resentment just waiting to explode on that dreadful evening.*

*Quite,* I agreed, cutting a dainty piece of scone with my knife and relishing its crumbly texture in my mouth as I did so.

In reality, I would have chosen to substitute 'retribution' for 'resentment' in that last sentence of hers, but deemed it wiser to keep mum.

She's black. Celena. With one of those pale, almost translucent skins some of them have. Seriously white teeth. And loads of charm, I think, if only she could relax. In her line of work, I don't suppose she gets many laughs during office hours, so I understood her apprehension and was glad I'd put her at her ease.

She accepted the invitation of a lift in my taxi when our tête-à-tête was over and I dropped her off on St Mary's Street. No doubt she spent the rest of the afternoon writing up my case history and, like a prized possession, filed me proudly under 'Yes – Professional Men Beat Up Their Partners Too!' At least, I hope that's where she filed me. I wouldn't want to be just put in amongst the *hoi polloi*.

Even victims have their pride.

Saying this out loud in court is not allowed, it seems. The judge looks ominously over his glasses, halting the proceedings momentarily. It really is only for a moment, but I've learnt from day one that such pauses have a dramatic effect in court.

During the lull, my shrewd little barrister also points a discreet but piercing glare my way. I determine to heed her warning and return to ground rules.

It isn't easy. Even though the 'frail but unbroken' image has served me well enough up until now, the cut and thrust of cross-examination has tested it to the limits.

I broke down once, which is expected, apparently. Felt quite distressed at doing it. And was taken down for five minutes. Given water. The usual fussing around.

My hanky was bone dry. But I don't think those security people noticed – and I made sure it was well hidden away again in my handbag by the time I said I was well enough to continue and re-emerged in the well of the court. I know I mustn't do that again or it will be seen as a cop-out from facing the questions. Once is interpreted as being human and distressed and is perfectly natural. Even to be commended. But any more use of the waterworks is taken as histrionics. Or so I've been told. There's an art to all these rituals. Or at least a skill. And I'm jolly lucky that I'm a quick learner.

At the end of this afternoon, she of the wig and motherly bosom also tells me I must stop referring to learned counsel for the prosecution's questioning as, *This cut and thrust*. It could be interpreted as a callous throw-back to the deed of which I'm accused, it seems.

I tell her everyone in that place is obsessed with Tom's death.

*Well! It is rather a grave matter,* she retorts, *and the reason why we're all there. But don't worry. I'm sure we'll soon have you walking away from the whole ghastly business.*

She gives me confidence. I feel we're on the same wavelength.

It's official! I can walk away. I've been acquitted.

Old Whitfield turned out to be a real star. Stood at the top of the courthouse steps and read a speech: *On behalf of Mrs Jones and her family,* as the saying goes. He did it with great *gravitas* and when I saw it all earlier on the television there was a caption at the bottom of the screen with his name on it, and 'Mrs Belinda Jones' solicitor' written underneath. Daisy and I could be seen standing just behind him, slightly to his right, looking suitably relieved and still sombre at the same time. I looked straight ahead; Daisy's head was bowed. We both looked dignified.

*My client and her family are clearly relieved by the outcome of these harrowing court proceedings and delighted that this ordeal is behind them. One of the greatest sources of strength Mrs Belinda Jones has found to sustain her during the anguish of recent months has been the growing realisation that many other women, even more unfortunate than herself, still have to endure similar traumas to the one she herself has had to endure. Although hoping for a period of peace to come to terms with the tragedy which has befallen her, and to rebuild her own life, she urges society to ask why these criminal charges continue to be brought against people who are clearly the victims of domestic violence...*

They cut him off in his prime at that point – oh, how the old duffer was relishing his moment of glory! – and went into a studio discussion with someone from the Crown Prosecution Service and a marriage counsellor.

No sooner was I off those steps than I was whisked by car to some posh hotel in a corner of the city centre I never go. *We couldn't afford the Red Dragon Resort,* said Celena cuttingly. We have a rapport.

It was a press conference, would you believe it? My first.

I'd told myself beforehand to continue to behave as though I was still in court and I was still in that ghastly beige two-piece and yellow blouse I've worn to court most days. Well-tailored to carry my status and style, but drab enough to seem downtrodden at the same time. Hand-picked after consultations with Whitfield and my barrister, it certainly did the trick in court. And at the hotel also, the scene was set for me to continue to be articulate but measured in my responses. Tom was given a thorough going over. Again. I'm detailed, but careful not to sound vindictive. Once the first few questions are dealt with, I relax and start to enjoy myself. I try to deflect the questions away from my own case – thus making me seem more concerned about others than myself and, therefore, rather kind.

I surprised myself at how easy it was to pull it off.

Everyone from Women's Aid are delighted with my performance.

*Victims are rarely as eloquent as you,* Celena enthuses afterwards. *Your story really captures the imagination and brings it home to the middle classes. You sure are a real find.*

This pleases me no end. Not the fact that 'my story' will clearly be spread all over the papers and TV news services again tomorrow, as it has been for several weeks – *that* I have loathed with a passion throughout the trial – but that I'm considered 'a real find'. This is something I have not been before.

There was some talk of a conference in Harrogate in December before we all parted and other 'chats' to women's groups the length and breadth of Britain. There's something of a circuit, apparently. And I could be on it.

When Mummy rang earlier, all she really had to say was, *Well done!* It felt as though I'd been given a gold star for a painting by a teacher in primary school.

Daddy went one better with, *Well! You've done it again.*

I assumed he meant I'd got away with it. And perhaps he's right.

*You always were a one for winding up men,* he adds with a chuckle.

It's one of the few natural talents I ever had, I want to say back to him. But sensing that it sounds too self-satisfied on a day like today, I refrain.

They're both old, that's the trouble. They both wish I'd married Rod. They both know I only broke off the engagement because Tom started showing an interest and I thought he'd be a better catch. They know what I'm like, but only allow themselves to be judgemental by proxy.

Daddy's gout is worse and there were heavy hints tonight that I should go down to stay with them for a few weeks, *Since there's no longer any danger of you going to clink.*

Daisy surprised me earlier by asking should she take down all her father's pictures dotted around the house. I hadn't really noticed them. Which even strikes me as strange. It is as if I am a stranger here. Suddenly, I find that this whole house awaits my rediscovery. In fact, it simply awaits my presence. It is as if I had never been here before. Rooms are familiar. That is true. Their layouts and effects are known to me. But I inhabit them with detachment. And even in the kitchen, I am able to hum a tune and turn the kettle on with impunity, as though nothing momentous had ever happened there.

It's been a week. And still I haven't ventured into town, sensing that here I'll always be vilified for taking away old Dr Tom.

Daisy and Rhiannon are coming for the day tomorrow. They want to cut the lawn and do, *A lotta stuff that needs doing*. They'll also bring me some supplies. I'll cope 'til then. Coping is something I do well.

The pictures have gone. I think Daisy was right. Tom's image has been vanquished into albums. There he is allowed to linger on, but he no longer shows his face around here. The mantelpieces and window-sills look fine without him. A part of me feared the house would look empty – but it doesn't.

Most of my regrets are about Daisy, really. Not Tom.

I'd never wanted one of those 'we're more like friends than mother and daughter' relationships which are all the rage these days. Those ghastly television programmes have them on all the time; both generations usually as uninhibited as each other – bra straps showing as they discuss contraception or go out drinking together on the pull. Well! Frankly, it just isn't me, those hideous blurring of the lines. If I'd wanted to made new friends all those years ago, I'd have joint a pottery class. Instead, I chose to do my duty and conceive.

All this, I now find I can tell her. Not in a 'we need to talk' frame of mind. And certainly not in confrontational mode any more, either. We converse. And things get said. And although there's very little hugging, we are, at least, at last relaxed

together. As Rhiannon would have it, I suppose we really are
'all girls together' now.

Major *faux pas* at the very start tonight. The anorexic in the
pleated skirt who's doing the honours – she thinks she's
making some ironic statement but only manages to make
herself look ridiculous – introduces me as Dr Belinda Jones.

When I get up, my eyes are peeled on my little laptop, as
usual, ready to take my cue from my *aide-mémoire*. But before
I've even focused properly on the writing on the screen, as I
normally do to overcome my nerves, I find myself saying that
the only doctor who was ever a part of my family was my
husband. *And he's dead,* I add. *I killed him.*

The response to these words falls into two very distinct
camps. Some audibly gasp and I feel a chill wind blowing
towards me. Others chuckle in what I can only perceive to be
admiration. There is actually some applause.

Perversely, I am not fazed by this diversity. Rather, it seems
to me, my confidence is boosted. I want to court both camps.
Both the approving and the disapproving have a role to play
in my buoyancy.

I want to abandon my usual little message of hope and tell
it as it really was.

I want to say I'm sorry.

I want to say that Tom did not deserve to die the way he
did. No one could possibly deserve to die such a sordid,
unintentional, insignificant little death as that.

He hadn't been at his worse that evening. Not by a long
chalk. He hadn't even been home long. I just happened to be
in the kitchen. The fish-gutting knife just happened to be out
because they happened to have some lovely-looking trout in

69

the market that day. I'd been there at the kitchen sink when he came home.

I knew immediately that it had been one of his drink-sodden afternoons at Gerald's. Gerald and Millie were supposedly our best friends. He's another doctor, with much the same predilections as Tom. They both smoked like chimneys and Gerald is also a boozy old bore – if not actually alcoholic like Tom. I'd often suspected over the years that Millie also bore the brunt of his wrath from time to time, as I did from Tom, but then again, she'd never had the same need for good sunglasses as I had. And I certainly never raised the matter with her. It was dinner and, *Darling, how lovely to see you!* and the very occasional game of golf sort of friendship. No more. I never could abide that ridiculous jet-black colour she dyed her hair.

He'd been at their house all afternoon. *Having a professional chin-wag,* Gerald proclaimed in court when he took the witness stand for the prosecution.

Well! I knew full well what that meant. Doctors are the worse on God's earth for opening bottles and passing round the cigarettes as they pontificate on what's best for everyone else's lungs and livers. Hypocrites extraordinaire. Every last one of them. Well, most of them. The ones Tom associated with, for sure.

Gerald admitted that the alcohol consumption had been pretty high that afternoon, but seemed positively horrified at the suggestion that Tom could have been cantankerous or agitated. Oh! How he pushed out that chest of his as he tried to impress the jury with his integrity.

The car was left there. Tom took a taxi home. There was no denying that. The taxi driver was a most sympathetic chap who said Tom had been arrogant and slurring – two vices that do not make for pleasant company when they are combined.

Antagonising factor number one was the smell of fish. He let it be known that he did not appreciate it.

I smirked in response, apparently. Antagonising factor number two.

By the third, I'd stopped counting and was fighting for my breath as he tried to choke me, my head being battered against the freezer where I'd hoped to place the trout before Tom's return – another domestic task I'd clearly failed to adequately complete.

Now, up 'til then it had been fairly mundane. Yes, my hair was dishevelled and my brow bruised, but none of this was really out of the ordinary during such scenarios.

It was the assertion that I had been hormonally programmed to put up with such indignities which finally sealed his fate. I found it an affront to my common sense, this supposedly foolproof research he spouted. Some women, apparently, have a genetic disposition to stoicism. They want to feel that they are simply 'putting up' with a given situation because it satisfies some deeply held need within them to feel thus.

He was suddenly absurd. And although I'd found him to be many things over the years, he had never been that before.

*Oh, dear! Look what my hormones made me do now!* That's what I felt like saying immediately after doing it. But I didn't, of course. I said nothing. I could barely breathe. Just wondered what had happened to the teak handle which I'd clasped so tightly a moment earlier. (I like the feel of good wood. I always have.)

Then I see it. It's pointing at me though the shirt, which is still mostly white. And then I notice the blooded hand print on the hob. Thank God I hadn't recently had it on – he would have had a nasty burn.

The purple, which his face had been as he exhaled his fumes an inch or so away from mine a moment earlier, suddenly turned a brighter red, as though some hitherto undiscovered supply of blood had rushed to those veined cheeks.

I massage my throat, trying to convince myself that I'm still breathing; half wishing that I wasn't.

It isn't until he staggers slowly to the floor – and this takes what seemed like an extraordinarily long time – that the magnitude of the situation dawns on me. Still, I say nothing. Neither does he. But I sense that he has never sobered up so quickly. It is a rare moment of united serenity between us. And I realise it is our last together. Our last together! I can actually think these thoughts.

I slide my hand across the slimy draining board and bend over as though I am gasping for breath. I *am* gasping for breath.

The three remaining fish drop into the sink. It is, after all, a domestic scene and it is the ordinariness of what has just happened which horrifies me. More than the actual loss of life. And even then, there, at that moment of horrendous blackness, as I gasp and stare into a void of sheer terror, I know that I shall not actually tell that thought to a living soul.

Realising that I must summon help, I am consumed with fear at the thought of leaving him there on the floor. My mobile is upstairs. Our landline receiver in the lounge next door. I don't want to let him out of my sight. I remember how that man in *Halloween* kept coming after Jamie Lee Curtis, even after he should logically have been long since dead. It's absurd. And for a fleeting moment, very, very real.

I don't want to loose sight of him there – not out of any sense of gloating glee, but pure petrifaction. His eyes never really closed. I can only surmise that the medics did something to them after they came. (I also never saw that knife again until it was produced in court. How some of the minutiae come to haunt me even now, a year later! I never got it back. I wonder where it is?)

My sticky, smelly, guilty little fingers eventually dialled calmly on the landline receiver and I spoke with clarity.

*Can you feel a pulse?* he asked. I wanted to ask if he was trained to sound so detached in what must be a stressful job. Or had he simply cultivated a self-defence mechanism over time?

I had to force myself to think what a pulse was for a moment. Going back into the kitchen, I finally realise that Tom no longer has one. And that he did not deserve.

No one can deserve that. Tom didn't. He was a most unhappy man.

Naturally, none of this is spoken to the gathered throng. What they get in the end is the usual little speech, dictated by the bullet points which come up on the laptop, about my Home Counties upbringing, my private education and my marriage. Oh, yes! They get the marriage. They even get some of Tom's background. How he was expected to follow his father into medicine. How he felt inadequate compared to the old man's eminence. How, despite the fact that he loathed that venomous little town, he had an ingrained need to give something back to the community. (An aspiration with which I had never been burdened.)

I paint this picture of incompatibility, but say very little about the suffering I endured.

73

During the 'your chance to ask a question to our guest speaker' sequence which inevitable follows, I'm asked the obvious: why did I stay with him?

I say it's for Daisy (which is most commendable). And for the status (which isn't, but at least I'm being honest). I don't mention the deriving of some perverse joy from taking the moral high ground. Or wanting to avoid the sheer indignity of admitting defeat. And I certainly don't mention hormonal dependency.

All those I keep to myself.


True celebrity status at last. I was on *Woman's Hour* today. A full five minute interview to myself. No other victims taking part. No 'experts'. Just me. And I'm tickled pink.

They only rang two days ago. (Not much forward planning involved for these people, it seems.) And luckily they tracked me down here, to my parents' house – so going up to central London wasn't half the trek it would have been from Wales.

The minion who first contacted me was male, which rather surprised me at the time. But I made no comment. Called himself a researcher. Some recently-graduated whiz-kid with aspirations of being Director General, I thought. He explained that this new report had been published. Made rather a meal of taking me through the salient points. Would I like to comment?

Before I have a chance to say I'd love to come on their little programme, he chips in with a personal opinion, namely that it's perfectly understandable that the police become involved in cases such as mine, because, *There has, after all, been a fatality.*

*I wish they'd felt compelled to involve themselves when I was being battered,* I raged back at him. Twice, over the years, Daisy had run to her bedroom and rang them on her mobile. Not once had I seen them exactly blazing a trail to our well-varnished door, all sirens sounding!

He didn't mean to be insensitive, he insisted. And he certainly didn't mean to imply that it was right that I was charged with manslaughter.

*It was murder initially,* I told him.

*Oh, yes! Quite! I know,* he fumbled.

What did he suggest would have been an appropriate charge for me, I asked. *Causing a disturbance in a kitchen?*

I could easily have pleaded guilty to that one, I felt like adding. Well! There was an awful mess.

Silence. And I feel sure he'll think twice before offering anyone an opinion in future.

I, for my part, had no such qualms today. They introduced me as being at the centre of, *The most high-profile case of its kind in recent years.* And even though I say so myself, I think I gave them value for money. As I left the studio, the boy-wonder researcher told me he felt almost sure that there'd be a 'lively response' to what I had to say on their website.

Rhiannon texted me – which is good of her, given all the circumstances. Daisy rang.

The moment my mother realised who was on the line she handed me the receiver. Daisy is very much in the doghouse for the time being. It seems she and Daddy had rather taken to old Rhiannon and are taking her side in our little family's latest upheaval. They have always taken an uncharacteristically puritan line on any form of infidelity. So there's that for them to cope with, coupled with the fact that they can't understand why anyone would dump a nurse for a car mechanic. I've tried to explain to them that both occupations are very necessary in their different ways, but to no avail. And in truth, I'm with them all the way. A grease monkey with tattoos who constantly moans about her heavy periods is not what I dreamt of as a son-in-law.

Today saw the zenith of my brush with fame, I think. Travelling back here to my parents' home, it dawned on me how weary I've become of getting to all those obscure little places with my story. It's all worn a little thin. And I've grown very tired of all that driving. The traffic can be murder. That's why today, I took the train.

You can still smell the paint. But Daisy won't mind. She'll only be here for the one night.

It's all happened so quickly in the end. Her being accepted as an international volunteer. Me finding a buyer at last for the house in Abertrisant. The decision to move back. (Surrey has always really been my home.) Finding this apartment.

She'll approve of it, I hope. Daisy. Not that she's really understood my need to move away from Wales. And God knows I've tried to explain it several ways. *Your grandparents live a couple of miles away – it will be so much easier for me to keep an eye on them,* was my latest line of argument. And probably my feeblest to date.

*Why bother? They won't be with us long,* was her immediate reply. She shot me down, dead.

The young are so matter-of-fact about everything. And they're right to be so, of course. She'll see things my way, given time. And in the meantime, if she's decided to squander her new found wealth on being Mother Theresa for a year, I have to support her, of course. I don't regret giving it to her.

Half the profit from the house sale was only fair. It had, after all, been her home.

After I take her to Dover tomorrow, I shan't see Daisy for a full year. (My first thought on hearing this was that the mechanic's ardour was sure to wane in that time. Now I'm not so sure what's been going on. I'm on the outside, wondering. The way all mothers do, I suspect.)

She'll be in Paris for a month, it seems. All training programmes take place there, apparently, before they're sent to India.

It's to do with some irrigation scheme. The main thrust of her work over there. If I've understood it correctly, which I probably haven't. And she'll do some teaching. Which made me laugh.

*God knows where you'll get the patience from,* I told her.

*Yes, I expect he does,* she answered.

She hasn't found religion. It's just her way of trying to wind me up.

Our only daughter has become a do-gooder. Regrets not doing it straight from university, so she now claims. Thinks half the money from the house, which I've given her, will give her the financial stability she needs to really 'do her own thing'. Well! There are things we all regret not doing straight from university, I want to tell her. But I don't, of course. Because in my instance, it would mean she wouldn't be here at all.

Despite my reservations, she's determined to go out and do her bit among the fly-infected squalor of some far-flung hell-hole.

*Giving something back to humanity,* she calls it.

Her father would be proud of her.

# Rowena's Last Rant

Rowena had to be fully accessorized, even for death. To face such a significant encounter clutching the wrong handbag or wearing a pair of gloves not fully co-ordinated with the rest of her outfit simply wouldn't do at all. Not for Rowena.

Frail and nearly seventy, she was riddled with most of life's afflictions. Except guilt. To that, she seemed immune, as she had been all her life.

Her almost fleshless cheeks were be-rouged to such a crimson degree they seemed to ridicule the embalmer's art before he'd even had a chance to get to work.

Lori, charged with her care for the night, feared the worse. She was untrained and mostly uncommitted to the job, but Mrs Pritchard's final words before leaving had been that she held her responsible for Rowena... and no, there wouldn't be any extra money in it for her.

'It's the wrong shade,' insisted Rowena, with an unnervingly strong voice for a woman not expected to make it through the night. The offending article was removed from her invisible lower lip and handed back to Lori with an uncertain aim. 'More voluptuousness. Bring me more voluptuousness.'

The use of such a defiant vocabulary was quite fitting for a *femme fatale* on her deathbed, thought Lori. She herself was well-acquainted with defiance and laughed a little on the inside, uncertain whether it was from contempt or admiration towards the old woman.

She focused on black, because black was voluptuous in Lori's eyes. It's what she always wore.

Striding assertively over to the dressing-table, she rummaged for the nearest she could find to black, among the lipsticks that had spewed forth from Rowena's clapped-out vanity case. She took her time, well aware that she would be kinder towards the old girl with colours than she ever could be with words.

'Too dour,' rebuked Rowena on having Lori's latest choice placed in her hand. 'I want curves... and colour.'

'Purple is a colour.'

'Don't get smart with me, lady. You're only a paid servant, you know.'

'So you keep reminding me.' Lori's tone told the world that the ambivalence she'd experienced moments earlier had quickly given way to bitter contempt. The world, however, was but one room. And Rowena was its only resident.

In truth, Lori hated her work. She loathed the fact that she was merely a curator in a museum of human dereliction. This is what passed as employment for her. She resented the occupational requirement to feign compassion from time to time. In truth, she wanted no part of the demolition process which passed as 'care for the elderly' in this houseful of ramshackled relics.

'Mummy always said one should keep a distance from staff. It never pays to fraternise.'

'We never listened to Mummy though, did we, Rowena?' Lori gloated, lowering her head and her voice towards the pillow in the guise of one who cared.

She didn't care. Not really. She knew this was fundamentally wrong, but she'd seen it all before. Or so she thought. The night shift was usually easy money for what it was worth. Mrs Pritchard always insisted that the last resident be in bed by nine and Lori could then sit down in the basement kitchen of this once-imposing house and text her lover with her feet up on the Aga and the Walkman in her ears.

No one died here. They just faded. Usually removed discreetly to a hospital when the end was near.

'Don't think you'd have lasted a week in the old days,' said Rowena, her voice defiantly clear and cultured, filling her final room with her disdain. 'Not even as a chambermaid... never mind as anything else.'

'Hard taskmaster, was she, your mother? At this hotel of yours.'

'Standards. That's what we had then. Family-run, you see. Not some huge conglomerate. Not like now.'

'Not on the prom, though, was it? Your hotel.'

'There was a sea view,' Rowena insisted. The venom in her voice touched the four corners.

Despite herself, Lori couldn't help but admire the pride that exuded from the deathbed before her, as much as she ridiculed the futility of it all.

'I could have skivvied for you, like I have for everyone else all my life,' she joked half-heartedly. 'I'm good for that, so I'm told.'

'Don't start playing the hard-done-by with me. You lesbians are all the same. Huge chips on your shoulders, always.'

'Overgeneralising, aren't we, Rowena?'

'Generalities are all you have with which to relate to the public in the hotel trade, my dear girl.'

Lori thought Rowena made the hotel trade sound like a branch of show business, which it probably was, but would not allow herself a smile at the sentiment.

'We welcomed everyone. You had to, you see. In those days. As long as they were respectable. Or at least discreet. And had the means to pay, of course.'

'Oh yes,' laughed Lori. 'That most of all, I would have thought.'

'The Royal Snowdonia, my dear girl. That's what we were called. The name goes back to Victorian times. And it meant more to us than just a business. Not like that hard-nosed common piece that owns this shit-hole.'

'Mrs Pritchard, you mean?'

'Llandudno's finest,' Rowena continued to reminisce, oblivious to Lori's point of detail. 'Llandudno's finest... in its class.'

'In its class,' mocked Lori. 'In its day. Not now. It's where they put all the DHSS rabble now. All those wino Scousers you see out on the prom all day, 'cause they get kicked out and haven't got the gumption to do anything else with their lives, or go anywhere else except the pubs. Definitely in a class of its own now, your Royal Snowdonia.'

Rowena, too weak to launch a full attack, chuckled contemptuously at her tormentor. 'Such a cheap jibe....'

'Times change. That's all.'

'Not our Royal Snowdonia any more. When we sold up, we begged them to change the name – those new owners – in case any of our regular clientele from years ago happened to be passing through and were tempted to book in for the night.'

'They'd have a shock if they did, wouldn't they?'

'Oh! They would, my dear,' Rowena rallied with some warmth. 'We always had fresh flowers on the desk in reception, you know.'

'So you told me.'

'Did I? Yes, I suppose I did.... Is the doctor coming?'

'Doctor saw you this afternoon, Rowena. Remember?'

'Did he?'

'Nothing more he can do, see. You're not in any pain and we're just to keep you comfortable... "for the duration". Those were his very words, according to Mrs Pritchard.'

Rowena had stopped listening. Words hurt her now. Not their meaning, but their sound. They were dull aches that drained still further her dwindling power of consciousness. When she'd reluctantly agreed to move to this place three months earlier, she'd taken solace in the fact that it called itself a 'rest home'. *I'm not a nursing case, you see? Or Murray would have found me a nursing home, wouldn't he? I just need rest, that's all.*

In reality, she'd known precious little rest here. She'd seen even less of Murray. It was as if her very flesh had rapidly been consumed by the institutionalised conformity of her last address and the conspicuous absence of her only son.

Blame the place! Blame the system! Blame other people! *It's never your fault, is it, Rowena?*

The right hand, having let the latest offending lipstick roll from its grasp, made a stab at combing its skinny fingers through her hair. It failed.

Her moistened eyes flared with frustration. It had looked such a mess the last time she'd seen herself in a looking-glass. Her once immaculate *coiffure* has died before her on the pillow. With the roots showing.

*Always someone else's fault, Rowena. Never yours.* It was true. But her mother could chirp as much as she liked. If she and Daddy hadn't left such a mess, she wouldn't have had to pay all those death duties which ate away at the profits of the hotel sale. ·

Three rooms in the end. Having once ruled over thirty-two. Plus bridal suite. Three dingy rooms and the Great Orme looming at the back, cutting off the light, even on the sunniest days.

She hadn't felt the tear. Only now, Lori was wiping something rough across her eyelids. And suddenly, she realised why. And what.

One room now. Single occupancy. No pets.

*Room service! The end delivered softly. No tip expected. Gratuities are always at the customer's discretion.*

*It's only the hotel angel doing his duty. Unobtrusive. Universal. Uninvited guest. He has come to turn life over. Give him nothing. He will take what is his soon enough. This is Death en suite, Rowena dear. Sign in. Check out.*

'The chambermaids always stole from guests, you know. Given half a chance.'

'Surely not? Not from such a well-run establishment as yours, Rowena?'

'No, not all, of course. Daddy always warned Mummy against generalising so. You have to be fair, you see.'

'Of course you do.'

'All the casuals stole,' Rowena soldiered on through her memories without further thought. 'Not so much the long-stayers. Some stayed for years. They did, back then. But all those wretched students we had to get in over the summer months. They were worse...'

'Watch it! My girlfriend's boy is a student. Lancaster University. Doing Maths. That's the only reason why I do this,' said Lori sternly. 'To put him through college.'

'Do you love her very much?' Distracted by the thought of love, Rowena's voice gathered warmth again and resonated with just a hint of envy.

Lori made no reply.

'Wish I'd met her. Is she nice?'

'You'd like her. She's kinder than me.'

'I should have been a lesbian.'

Misinterpreting a profound disclosure as merely a sign of dementia, Lori completely misjudged the moment and could only mock, 'Good gracious, Rowena. You are a one! Whatever will you shock me with next?'

'I think most women would be if we weren't all so easily distracted. First sight of a decent prick and we're off. The crushes of our youth all but forgotten.'

Lori laughed out loud. Not something she was famous for.

'The guests nicked too,' Rowena continued, her lack of timing as ignoble as Lori's lack of sensitivity. 'The Scousers and the blacks were the worst – ashtrays mostly.'

The sudden blush of liberation the laughter had induced in Lori's cheeks was quelled in an instant. These two women would not venture closer this night. Their moment had passed.

'Most hotel rooms these days are non-smoking, Rowena.

That must have put paid to that little habit.'

'Towels, too. And sheets sometimes. Merseyside must be awash with linen from north Walian hotels.'

'Is that what Mummy said?'

Rowena heard the voice, but not the words.

'The kitchen hands were worse of all. Much worse.'

'Did one of them seduce the proprietor's daughter?'

'Seduced...' Rowena started. Then nothing more could come. Only those recurring tears. Choking those once resplendent eyes.

*Up the spout. The shame of it all.*

Is this what it was really meant to be like? This passing? A collage of colour? Vibrant and voluptuous? At the tip of her dried-up tongue? Glistening? Moistening? A lip-gloss lustre life? Left, kiss-shaped, on the looking glass? That brazen Sixties defiance that defined her life for over forty years was back in her mouth like a taste she was destined to take with her to eternity. A toothpaste taste.

She remembered. Horror of horrors! She remembered.

She remembered how she'd stood up to her parents and adamantly refusal to either abort or opt for adoption. It had been a defining time in her life. Despite its seemingly admirably heroic nature, it had been both defining and defeating.

She'd been beautiful then. And Rowena knew what price there was to pay for beauty.

*Mummy cried and then took charge.* Of course she did. Of course. She took charge of everything.

'You must despise me, my dear. You do, don't you?'

'No I don't,' Lori replied without conviction.

'My straight talking has always been respected,' claimed

Rowena, 'even by those who hated my guts.'

'Is that really what you think? Personally, I think you've just been pitied all your life,' judged Lori. 'That's the impression I get from the few who've rang to ask after you that I've spoken to. Those few so-called "friends".'

Rowena wanted to retort with a customary, *How dare you?* But even instinct was deserting her now. Turning her face to the side, her still-watering eyes only allowed a muffled view of pillow cover.

'I wish I'd had a strong woman friend in my life. One who'd have stuck with me. One who wouldn't desert me now.'

'I thought you had,' said Lori.

'Murray is an arsehole,' she proclaimed. Her voice was strong again but there was no coherence with what had gone before. 'Wears Versace suits and cons his way around London calling himself a 'leisure facilities consultant'.'

'Now, Rowena, don't upset yourself, love.'

'I know what you're up to...Thieving bitch!'

In the few weeks she'd been in residence, Rowena knew that several things had gone missing. Dignity. Gone. Independence. Gone. Memory. *Now where the hell did I put that? Oh, yes! I remember.* It's gone.

It would all be missing soon. A cold clandestine hand hovered over her life's trinkets. Ready for the taking.

*Hotel angel, pray for me now and at the hour of my wake-up call.*

Down on the reception desk at The Royal Snowdonia, right next to the vase, they always had a bowl of enormously large mints – the sort on which a child could easily choke. They had been offered as salvation to any halitosis victim who happened to be passing through and their taste came back to haunt

Rowena for a moment, strong and smooth.

*Do take one as a parting gift. They are complimentary. Goodbye.*

In many ways, Lori started to feel that she wanted to be like Rowena. Not the delusion of grandeur which had marked her life. Nor the financial struggles which had marred her later years. And she certainly didn't want that look of a 'last-chance saloon girl' she had tonight. The muck which was, it seems, to pass for glamour on Rowena's face and nails right up to the very end, appalled her. Apart from drag queens, Lori had never seen cosmetics so copiously applied to gild the chaos of a life. And yet, inside, for private consumption only, she had to acknowledge a strange regret that her attempts at fulfilling Rowena's desire for an immaculate parting image hadn't quite succeeded in masking the mayhem of everything which had gone before.

Despite the mixture of repulsion and regret by which she was consumed, she wanted to be a little like Rowena. Not dead, exactly. But bitter to the end.

Rowena died with her mouth still open, as if there were more to come. About Murray and Mummy; thieving guests and grasping taxmen; impressive pricks and unrequited love. Her eyes, in contrast, had closed with the drawing of that last breath. And her jaw took upon itself the prominence of a pier.

Hovering above, unknown to either the deceased or her carer, one sleepy seagull cooed its aubade in that seaside confusion between mist and dawn.

When Lori finally crept into bed, it was still warm from her partner. She'd noticed in the kitchen that the water in the kettle was still relatively hot; toast crumbs on the lounge carpet still fresh. They must have missed each other by minutes.

Long nights called for deep sleeps and Lori longed for hers. The lingering fragrance of a woman more overtly feminine than herself lulled her from the overbearing burden of the night's events.

Hadn't Mrs Pritchard hurried from her own home to her so-called 'rest home' as soon as Lori rang? She'd obviously been half awake, expecting the call. The doctor immediately summoned, so the death certificate could be signed and the corpse taken away without delay. She had wanted Rowena removed before the others got up for breakfast and the day staff had already been instructed to eradicate all evidence of her existence before curtains were drawn.

Much to their delight, someone else's happy relatives would no doubt have been informed of the vacancy by now. Lori knew that the room was already allocated. Bags were hurriedly being packed even as she drifted towards sleep, so that another family's burden could be dumped into Mrs Pritchard's care 'for the duration'.

On arriving to take charge of the situation at around seven, Mrs Pritchard had done what was necessary to Rowena's remains with an unnervingly detached balance between duty and disdain. This balance is what made her a successful business woman, Lori supposed. Mrs Pritchard's shabby taste in suits coupled with her efficiency in covering a lack of any genuine emotion towards anyone struck Lori as a wicked combination. Not good for being the head of any home. But great for ensuring material success.

Mrs Pritchard hated deaths in her homes and rarely allowed

them. Rowena had indeed been an exception. Lori had been present earlier in the evening as the doctor tried in vain to find a hospital bed. It had been like Christmas. A free bed was there none. Hence her vigil. Her 'one night only' twosome with redoubtable Rowena. What a duo! What a death!

As sleep slowly crept over her, like a less demanding version of death, Lori dreamt once more of getting close to a tall woman with a once-Titian head of hair and the lone scar reminder of an only son on her belly. Moaning quietly, halfway between an orgasm and a snore, she kissed away her disappointments in the dark.

# Sunset at Kastro's

Have you ever seen the sunset from Kastro's? You really ought to go sometime. The flight is long and the island remote, but it's well worth the effort.

Gweirydd was there to meet Marco. Or so he thought. It had only been some fifteen hours since he'd first met the young Italian. That had been in the heat of the night. Under a moon-lit sky. Over by the castle ruins, a stone's throw from the bar.

'I'll meet you tomorrow at Kastro's, to see the sunset,' had been Gweirydd's last words. They were virtually the only words of their encounter. Words are obsolete under the castle walls in the dead of night.

'*Ciao*, baby!' The words had come back at him through the sultry air.

He would recognise him again, wouldn't he? Of course he would! Surely? Gweirydd did his utmost to convince himself. His eyes kept vigil at the door, hoping he didn't draw too much attention to himself as he did so. He scrutinised all who descended the three steep steps which led down to the bar. Just in case. But so far, no one had even come close to resembling Marco.

Some twenty minutes earlier, when he first arrived and the bar had just opened for business, he'd avoided the large, imposing wooden seats which faced the window and the sea. Deliberately. He knew from many years' experience that they would soon be crowded. They offered the best views and were always commandeered by the most beautiful people.

He preferred to sit back, nearer the door, on a cushion-covered bench with the white-washed stone wall for a backrest. Every time he relaxed, his head hit the wooden mirror frame which hung above him. Occasionally, he'd pick up the long tall glass on the low table in front of him and sip slowly on his gin and tonic. The drinks were expensive and Gweirydd's pocket wasn't deep. He measured all his pleasures, like gifts from the gods. Treasuring them and making each one last as long as he could.

His eyes scanned the Americans who'd arrived shortly after him, and who'd long since colonised the prize possession sofas facing the window in anticipation of the nightly spectacle. Their fashionable clothes, muscular physiques and loud voices epitomised everything that made Gweirydd feel inferior. They exuded confidence and a casual assertion of their right to fun.

Gweirydd eavesdropped. Some talked of the beach they'd been on that day. Others mentioned home. Which state? Which city? Did they know there was no McDonald's on the island? Gweirydd knew. But he'd never heard it described as a tragedy before!

They were mostly divided into couples and had entered

separately in quick succession. Smiles, handshakes and a ritual exchange of names had all happened within seconds of them taking charge of the prime seats.

Fiddling with his shirt collar, Gweirydd diverted his eyes from the door for a moment. Although his clothes bore no designer labels, he didn't look out of place. He was slim and pleasant looking in a totally undistinguished kind of way. Blue shirt, grey trousers and a pair of brogues. This was Gweirydd in his holiday attire. Not dissimilar at all to that which he might have worn to the council office building where he worked back home in Wales.

Except that back home in Wales, of course, there would be no Marco. There'd be no Kastro's.

On a Friday night, he might venture down to the village pub and share a pint of beer with some so-called mates. On Mondays, he would definitely go to choir practice. On Sunday, chapel. Occasionally, he took part in poetry competitions and helped out with the local Young Farmers' Club – even though he'd never farmed in his life.

That was Gweirydd's life on the Llŷn Peninsular. He lived within his community's unwritten rules. Venturing occasionally to the seaside town of Llandudno, or beyond to the larger cities of England; Chester or Manchester. But never bringing his passion back home with him.

Not that he was naïve enough not to realise that most of his acquaintances had long since worked out he was gay. But he didn't want to rock any boats. That's why his annual holiday was his great escape. This fortnight of unrelenting indulgence as much a part of his recipe for a balanced year as the Cerdd Dant singing festival at which his choir took part every November or Christmas.

Suddenly, the mood in Kastro's was massaged by something by Mahler which Gweirydd couldn't quite place. It was one of the bar's peculiarities that only classical music was ever played there. Part of the overture from Carmen had set an exuberant tone when he first arrived, but now the sun was gently descending and was destined to die in mournful glory.

'Where are you from?'

Gweirydd was startled for a moment by the voice. So intense had been his door-fixated stare and his search through Mahler's repertoire, he hadn't even noticed the couple taking the double seat by his side.

He turned to look at them and looked away again immediately. New people were arriving all the time. An elderly couple struggled on the three steps and stopped the flow for a minute. Now was a crucial time. His eyes hurriedly surveyed the room in case Marco had slipped in without his noticing. But he hadn't. And Gweirydd sighed his disappointment.

'Wales,' he replied at last, the time he'd taken to answer masked by the lethargic ambience which prevailed. Ambience was all at Kastro's. The stillness of time. And beauty, of course. Beauty above all else. 'It's part of the United Kingdom,' he felt compelled to add with embarrassment.

'Oh, I know,' responded the woman most charmingly. She was black and tall and elegant. Her white teeth gleaming. Her clinging dress and the beads in her hair as tasteful and exotic as the rest of her. Exotic and expensive.

'Gwyneth is a Welsh name, is it not? As in Gwyneth Paltrow's name.'

Gweirydd would hardly call himself a film-buff, but luckily had heard of the actress. He awkwardly smiled his agreement. She carried on regardless.

'Gwyneth was the name of her mother's best friend in junior school and that's how she came to get the name. I read about it recently in *Hello!* magazine. It's a very unusual name in the States.'

It transpired that they weren't from the States at all, but Toronto. Except she wasn't even Canadian, but from Sierra Leone. Although Gweirydd was given their life story in a matter of minutes, no explanation was forthcoming as to how this beauty had escaped the impoverished hell of her war-torn homeland and was now partner to a middle-aged Canadian. He suspected a cheque-book was involved. But he didn't ask.

Still no sign of him. Marco. And the sun was fast tracking ever downwards towards its doom. If he didn't arrive soon, he'd miss the ultimate flamboyance. Gweirydd's eyes fleeted frantically between the horizon, the straight couple from Toronto and the door. Of the three, the door received the most glances. And still no Marco.

Then a totally insignificant man who'd been sitting on a stool opposite joined the conversation. Well, Gweirydd had dismissed him as a totally insignificant man. Now he was forced to look at him properly, he conceded that he was rather cute. Not his type, of course. Too short. Too old. But not without a certain attractive quality all the same.

He was Breton. Constantly mistaken for a Frenchman, apparently. He complained bitterly, much to the Canadians' amusement. Gweirydd sympathised and conceded that he too had to constantly explain that he wasn't English.

The Canadian smiles remained intact throughout. And since there were no American actresses exposed as having Breton names in *Hello!* magazine, it soon became apparent that the beauty from Sierra Leone had never heard of Brittany.

Gweirydd didn't really care that much. The forgotten peoples of minor nooks and crannies on the world map were really not what Kastro's was about. And frankly, although his Welshness meant so much to him, he'd never hankered after other Celtic connections. He could only cope with so much twilight.

The polite sedate exchanges between the four were momentarily drowned out by the raucous shrill of another straight couple sitting over at the other side. Their shrieking howls of laughter disturbed the serenity and the whole bar turned in unison to look at them in disgust. Despite the collective sense of ambience which seemed to always find a consensus in Kastro's, it was not a place where grudges were held. Once the look had been given, the point taken and the vulgarity subdued, everyone returned to their own level of reverential contemplation, either talking in groups or staring towards the imminent sunset.

No one had entered for a few minutes. Not a soul. An unusual lull in trade for Kastro's, where movement between the bar and the street was constant. He simply wasn't going to come, was he?

Gweirydd scowled openly for a moment, observing the offending loud-mouths opposite. She wore a pair of purple slacks with a floral top, while he was festooned in Hawaiian shorts and the most garish shirt he'd ever seen. God knows what the cocktails they had enthroned on the table before them contained, but needless to say, both drinks were multi-coloured.

Something by Chopin had taken over from Mahler. Yet again it had taken Gweirydd a while to notice.

Such changes weren't really meaningful here. Gweirydd

96

knew that well enough. Whenever a CD finished, one of the Greek boys behind the bar threw another one into the machine. Any significance was arbitrary, as was so often the case with any form of art.

But it was obvious that a lone piano would be the sun's accompaniment tonight as it bled its good-night along the skyline. And Gweirydd pictured a burning coin dropping into a cosmic slot machine – an image which appealed endlessly to the poet within him. It meant that each day was a gamble. It was essentially simplistic. And yet, tinged with the illusion of being an universal truth.

Watching the sunset at Kastro's was a significant moment for an insignificant poet, like Gweirydd.

And still, no sign of Marco!

It was an old disappointment. A gamble that hadn't paid off.

The place fell silent. The gay Americans. The wealthy Canadians. The verbose Breton. And Gweirydd himself. All mute for a moment. Tranquillised by the sense of inevitability. Almost tedious in its beauty it seemed. A sublime repetitiveness. This daily death across the water.

Only the three waiters continued with their duties, carrying trays and bringing change. Pretty boys well-trained to empathise with this transient trade.

All eyes focused on the huge windows. The end at last. That first kiss of sun and sea.

Gweirydd glanced in one last burst of anticipation. His eye had caught a movement at the door. It had only been two bearded men descending, their hushed voices barely touching the delicacy of the hour, before conforming to silence.

'Beautiful, isn't it?' Assuming, perhaps, that he had turned to look at her, the black woman had felt compelled to

97

speak. Gweirydd nodded, unable and unwilling to endorse the blandness of her remark in any other way.

How shallow she was after all! The prized possession of a shallow man.

He'd already gathered that she was a professional model and there seemed something egotistically perverse to him in the fact that she chose to holiday in one of the most photogenic places on earth. Did beauty crave beauty all the time? And if not beauty, money?

The sun had seemingly reformed. It was exactly halfway down; the symmetry with the sea's reflection creating a cruel illusion, like the swan song of a dying man.

The Breton, consumed with concern over the future of his own language and culture, started chatting again, having held his solidarity with silence long enough.

Two Bostonians seated nearby joined in. Neither had ever been to Europe before. This was their first visit – and Wales was on their itinerary. They would be there in a fortnight and were particularly eager to see Caernarfon Castle, it seems. Gweirydd refrained from mentioning that he lived but a few miles away. One was a lawyer; the other a computer expert. Both bore their beauty with confidence.

Would they be cruising later around the castle walls, wondered Gweirydd? It could be, if castles were their thing. Couples often did.

The lawyer was of Irish descent. A twinkle in his eyes. Pink dollar in his pocket. How Gweirydd envied him. This successful, surviving Celt. And when he called one of the waiters over to order another drink, he included Gweirydd and the Breton in the round. Another gin and tonic was on its way.

He hadn't really expected Marco to turn up, he convinced himself. No more than all the others over the years.

The sun had died again for another day. Out at sea, its remnants scattered debris over the sky, like a strawberry daiquiri in the haze.

The model and her man took their leave.

It would soon be night.

Gweirydd wouldn't stay much longer either. The second gin and tonic more quickly consumed than the first. He wanted to return to his hotel for an hour. A shower and an evening meal were in order before venturing forth to visit a few of the bars down at the quayside. All a diversion before his usual nocturnal stroll.

Tomorrow night, he'll probably be back at Kastro's for the sunset hour. Some other Marco expected to turn up, perhaps. Perhaps not. It didn't really matter. There was always a spectacular view of the sunset from here. And Gweirydd had learnt to take whatever comfort he could from the routine thrills of life.

At an appropriate time, when the Bostonians and the Breton were suitably engaged in conversation, Gweirydd took his leave, making his way towards the three steps and the door through which Marco never entered.

As he misplaced his footing on the second step, tragedy struck. Poor Gweirydd fell backwards, floating in slow motion through the musky air. In those seconds of descent he knew that this would be a clumsy death for such a sophisticated place. His head hit one of the heavy wooden table tops at quite the wrong angle. He knew it would. If there was one thing he'd learnt about Kastro's, it was its inevitability. The fracturing of his skull created a harsh, disruptive noise, sharply at odds with the gentle chatter which normally accompanied the ambience. His blood seeped upon the stone floor as his consciousness ebbed and waned for a while. The very colour seemed to parody the reason for the joint's popularity at this hour of the day.

People hurriedly removed their drinks from the vicinity and hovered in the vain hope of finding another seat, leaving the serving boys to figure out what should be done with such a strange anomaly.

Then, through the misty dusk of death, our dying Welshman saw a smart Italian descending the three steps, looking older than he had expected, but still unmistakably Marco. He'd made it after all. He'd come just in time to see the spectacular sunset he had been promised.

Gweirydd smiled at what he saw as a joyous revelation. It was almost biblical, he thought. Slightly sleazy. Very surreal.

Then he thought that to die in such circumstances would cause a stir back home. He imagined the glowing tributes paid him in his *papur bro* and felt them howling through his shattered brain; the hymns sung at his funeral a distant hissing in his ears.

None of this last disruption to Kastro's decorum is true, of course. It is only what Gweirydd most dreaded happening every time he left the bar. He is far too careful to ever slip. His life too controlled to ever falter. Gweirydd, of all people, is wise enough to know that he could never upstage the sun and that tonight, as always, he had already witnessed the only death that would ever be allowed at Kastro's.

He made it safely to the street. End of story.

# And the Nun Sails on...

It hadn't been a memory. Frustratingly, the paper really had slipped from his grasp. It had tottered on the edge, before finally sliding over the bedside. He hadn't had a clue. Well, he'd had the clues, but there had been no solutions. Words were fading fast. Even the Biro was proving unreliable. Faculties were bidding him farewell. The very stuff of life was rolling on the crest of a volatile wave. He was leaving land. The rock of certainty was almost out of reach.

No rage showed on his face as he sat there in his bed contemplating his predicament. He vaguely remembered holding the paper in his hands and staring with a pretend intelligence at the print, unable to register any meaning. Then it had gone. Like so much else. Gone.

Pain persisted, of course. There was always that. That was fundamental and even now, he knew it. But it was no longer allowed to be a comfort. They forbade him the experience.

Blocked it off at every corner with their pills and drips and injections.

Hospices were the ultimate maternity wards, he'd decided. They spelt confinement with a capital 'C'. They rendered Death as bland as possible. It was a modern movement. It was the modern way. Epidurals all round. All souls to sail towards eternity with as few ripples on the water as possible.

In this solitary room he felt more lonely than he had ever felt before. Old friends, such as books and delusions, had abandoned him, it seemed. Perhaps protocol had demanded that of them. The done thing. A necessary rite of passage.

He missed them for their own sake, to a degree. But in truth, it was the lack of stimulation that wounded him the most. The predictability of it all.

The staff, by common consent, were deemed wonderful by all and sundry. Their voices never rose above a certain pitch. Their smiles glowed with compassion, but were never radiant. No one ever asked, 'And how are you today?' after the customary 'Hello!' or 'Good morning'. Everyone already knew the answer. No one ever went there. Their discipline in this regard was a hallmark of their exemplary training.

They kept him looking nice, but in the staff room, well out of his earshot, they all muttered amongst themselves that he looked nothing like the distinguished poet he was meant to be.

When he was finally reunited with his copy of *The Times* that afternoon, it was courtesy of a care worker called Cathy who called into his room and picked it off the floor.

'I couldn't do them today,' he explained, referring to the cryptic clues.

'Never mind!' she responded, busying herself with the rearrangement of grapes in the bowl on the bedside cabinet.

Neatly folded, the discarded newspaper was unceremoniously placed on the empty surface by its side, where all others under her care displayed their greeting cards.

His only cards were in his mind. They were postcards, delivered by a damp dog he believed to be Death in disguise. It was an image too morbid to pursue with any relish and he knew he could no longer write it down. He could no long see the word 'dog' in his mind's eye. He only saw the dog.

'Would you like to go for a swim tomorrow morning?' asked Cathy. 'We could arrange it if you'd like.'

The absurdity of this suggestion was so enormous, it dwarfed his rapidly dwindling mental capability. He had heard that well-meaning 'friends' of the hospice had, some years earlier, committed themselves to the mammoth task of making something resembling a swimming pool materialise in the basement, but he had yet to see it. (Didn't he once donate a signed copy of one of his volumes that hadn't sold too well to an auction for this purpose? He couldn't well remember. Perhaps he really had. Or perhaps it was only his love of irony that now wished it had been so. Postcards often lied and told it as the sender wished it had been, he thought.)

'Maybe I should try it out,' his voice ventured weakly. The thought of limbs co-ordinating to achieve anything as physically coherent as a swim swept away confusion and left clarity sailing in serenity across a long forgotten horizon.

*Is the tide in tonight, in Aberystwyth? Or is it out? Something tells me it has a bearing on my life, but I cannot bring myself to care.*

*Do I already sense that sleep is never sweeter than when it follows good sex?*

Perhaps. Perhaps not. I am precocious enough for such arrogance at this age. I know I am by no means a stranger to deep sleep. Long before this night, my childhood has been awash with nights of blissful sleep. Those innocent, solo, single-bed sort of sleeps that are always cited as the bedrock of an idyllic childhood.

I am also already well-acquainted with sex. That adolescent road which leads to the joy of carnal exuberance has been well and truly travelled many times. But the strange truth is that I have never put these two pleasures together before. This is my first taste of that delightful drift into unconsciousness which comes from an empty sac and a happy heart. This is the first time I actually sleep with anyone.

Lovers, briefly, we are incompatible in all except our sexual desires. It is sex that sends us to sleep. It is sex that wakes us up. And in between, my first sublime taste of that soporific oblivion which congeals the senses of two whose limbs and thoughts are so intertwined they snore in unison, deep within their shared libido.

Eighteen and counting, this fateful first convergence of two renewals has come upon me unplanned and unannounced. His bed is already warmed. We have already made love once. It's late and I have no need to be anywhere else by any specific time tomorrow. All in all, to stay the night is not so much a decision, more an abandonment. I am lost in a sea mist of skin-smooth potency, half created by myself, half by him and half by fate. (I have always believed that every major 'first' in life is a feat of fate.)

I have inadvertently reached where I am meant to be this night.

Sleep is long. Not uninterrupted, but long. Its salt-tasting, *sweet-smelling comfort solving mysteries I have never dreamt existed and filling pits whose depths I have never fathomed. Sleep will never be the same again. Nor will sex.*

*Until now, sex has been an afternoon activity for me. Matinée performances with occasional hurried late-night encores. It is only in retrospect that I fully realise this.*

*He is older. Of course. They are always older. A fellow student with an attic room in a large Victorian house converted into student accommodation on the promenade. A so-called 'mature' student, his body is rounder, fuller and more firmly-formed than mine. Yet, to me he seems the seduced. Or is that arrogance on my part? His groans still echo in my mind, like the yelps of a covetous child, at last getting his hands on the toy he's lusted after for so long.*

*Sex has made the sea mute. I listen to silence. Only for a brief while can death-defying students be heard taunting the sea, running in and out of its clutches in their drunken state. This late-night din of drunken revelry momentarily encroaches upon our sleep; a distant, drowning symphony when all our seeds are spent.*

*Waking, somewhere in the night, the need to pee having dragged me away for a moment from that flesh which I've so overwhelmed and which has so overwhelmed me, I peep through thin curtains and hear the sea at last, its skin exposed as the mist withdraws silently in the distance. It glistens in the darkness and groaned slightly from what I think is love.*

\*

105

He waded ungraciously through the warm water, only temporarily invigorated by its undulating currents. His inaugural visit to the 'hydrotherapy pool' – as it was rather grandly called in the hospice brochure – had been a novel sensation, for which he was grateful, but the sense of exhaustion had returned like bitter recriminations to fuel an old feud.

He was dying. There was no escaping the fact. Maybe the 'therapy' was only meant to ease the tedium of the wait. It could do no other good, he thought. It had a palliative effect but he could not decide whether that was to be welcomed or not. He was fast becoming uncertain of the messages his body sent him. Deciphering subtleties was becoming difficult. All was lost in translation.

'Steady does it!' said Cathy from the safety of terra firma. She stood there with what seemed liked an enormous sail in an imaginary breeze. It was a towel and his frail body longed for its solace.

*I have walked along the promenade at Aberystwyth many times in the intervening years and often stopped to stare at all those upper windows, never knowing behind which one I discovered that lush, post-coital sleep.*

*The sea remained the same these fifty years and more. We didn't.*

He was no longer buoyant. The water over his face had the same effect as cleaning teeth with water from the wrong tap. He knew the warmth ought to be a comfort but, in the event, it only added to the sense of alienation.

'Steady does it!'

The voice behind him belonged to the male carer who had been his aquatic aide throughout this little escapade. Not being his type, he'd paid him scant attention. But suddenly, the stranger's strength was needed. He felt the one hand at his back and the other lifting his leg to reach the bottom step.

Being ex-military, this man's sense of detachment had always been seen as an asset by the hospice movement. To a poet on his last legs, however, his lack of any emotional commitment to the job seemed a rum affair. Still, almost despite himself, he muttered some words of gratitude. Manners had not always been important to him during his adult life, but now was a time for clutching at the time and tested tenors of one's upbringing. How the towel beckoned! He almost collapsed into Cathy's comfort.

*I awake to find a nun in close proximity to my face, staring down at me with grim curiosity. Encased in black, she hovers above me in Italian and nearly frightens me to death.*

*Here in Florence, a city of such incandescent light, the manufacturing of such man-made shadows seems a perverse attempt at simulated salvation. A poor show.*

*My soul is not shattered – only my leg.*

*Art liberates and fractures confine. This is a fine Florentine lesson to be learnt – with hovering nuns thrown in for good measure. However, I am already a practising masochist by now and well aware that pain encapsulates both. Not art and broken bones. But liberation and confinement.*

*Some minion from the diplomatic service has clearly been dispatched post-haste to enquire as to my well-being; his arrival at least relieving me of the old hag's curious scrutiny. He brings no grapes – a lamentable omission, which leaves me in no doubt at all that there must be some intended virtue to the austere circumstances in which I find myself. Even masochists want their creature comforts sometimes. In fact, this one wants* them often. Clearly, the Catholic Church and the British Council – which is responsible for my being in this city in the first place – have conspired to give me an authentic Renaissance experience in what is, after all, the quintessential Renaissance Town. (I make a mental note not to have anything to do with either organisation after this, but Florence itself I am prepared to forgive.)

Felicitations from the embassy and a brief round-up of all I have missed of Muse Celtique, due to my indisposition, are all the comfort he has to offer at this point and much to my own surprise, I find myself longing for the nun's return. At least she bears the trappings of benevolence amidst her misery.

With the shutters open, the ward I'm on is drenched in white. Several centuries of light have bleached the icons and religious artefacts that adorn these walls, dulling details of already half-obscured images in a manner which is comically reminiscent of bad dusting. I've been excused the cultural exchange, only to be submerged in my own subversions.

Before nightfall, my fellow Welsh ambassador to this festival of twilights – a softly-spoken woman who writes in Welsh and of whom I'd never heard before our flight together from Cardiff two days ago – did the decent thing vis-à-vis the grapes. She brought me some. Moreover, instinctively knowing not to tire a fellow poet with details of yet more poets' readings and discussion groups, proceeds to fill me in instead on the truly relevant rhymes and rhythms of life – who's ended up in bed with who, who got drunk last night and who caused a scene at lunch. Over the following few days – before being wheelchaired onto an aeroplane and flown home – we are to form a strong affinity. Throughout my life, I have found this rare among poets. Especially Welsh ones.

*The mystery man, it seems, has felt no such sense of fraternity. It is with glee that the police inform me that witnesses have seen him running from the wreckage of my hired car. They want to know his name and where I found him, as fleeing the scene of an accident is, it seems, as much a crime here as it is at home. Lying without an ounce of credibility in my voice, I tell the translator at my bedside that my concussion is much worse than first thought. This does nothing for my reputation as a poet of integrity but at least deflects all further questions regarding my anonymous motoring companion.*

*The embassy man coughs and, clearly delighting in my exposure as a dilettante, comments that local boys were never to be trusted. Bloody know-all!*

*For several days, the diplomat continues to bring papers for me to sign with all the joy of an executioner. The poet continues to bring grapes and gossip to consume. Otherwise, I remain uncraddled and unkissed, my temperament and fibula both left to recover by themselves.*

Inside, he tried to convince himself that the way he'd lived his life had held some meaning.

He awoke, shivering, still feeling his way through the imaginary water, taking comfort from the presence of the man behind him and the beckoning sail.

Suddenly, it dawned on him that he had endured the pain of self-relating in a more physical sense than most could understand or find acceptable. In desperation close to panic, he started questioning whether submitting himself to pain had ever been more than a cumbersome attempt at putting relationships into perspective? Perhaps it had. Perhaps not. Would his poetry have been more tortuous, and ultimately more liberating, had he not subjected himself to such sexual extremes in the real world? Had he debased his worth as a poet by choosing to physically suffer those torments he really should have put into words?.

'Do you think that using words to carry the inevitable burden of my sense of guilt would have been more expedient that putting my body in the front line?' How ludicrous he must sound! The thought he'd just uttered had been intended for private consumption only, but he soon realised that the words had somehow slipped out into the room, much to the bewilderment of the cleaner who had crept in to keep the dust at bay. Initially lost for an answer, she ended up disturbing no dust, but helping him with two clues of his crossword.

'We're all multi-skilling like mad here, Mr Davies,' she assured him. 'Now don't you worry no more 'bout them clues. Now is not the time for fretting.'

'Do I sound sanctimonious?' he asked her as she was about to leave. 'Saying all this now in hindsight?'

The broken bone in Tuscany had not been painless. It was the only broken bone he'd ever suffered throughout his life, but had been enough to convince him that he was not cut out for martyrdom.

'I should have put it into words instead!' he insisted. 'Don't you think? All that pain! I should have put it down. On paper. I should have put it into words!'

'We'll do some more tomorrow,' said the cleaner. 'Now don't you fret about them crossword clues. Sure, don't the devil do enough to bamboozle us already, without us inventing some more for ourselves and printing them in newspapers every day?'

*I have to be content with knowing that I inadvertently*

*introverted my art and perverted the integrity of both my words and my flesh. That is why neither will endure and why I have rendered myself unfulfilled in both media.*

Lying immobilised and plaster-bound in that half convent, half infirmary, all those Italian years ago, how he had amused himself by pondering the possibilities of the tables being turned on sublime artistic creations. Role reversal could negate all art, he'd thought at the time, and the perversity of it all returned to haunt him. What if the real, historic Macbeth had tried to capture the genius of Shakespeare, he'd wondered? And the people of Guernica had had a stab at paying homage to the torments of Picasso? Or the youth who modelled for David had taken his chisel out to attempt a likeness of Michelangelo?

Everyone could pretend they were equal now. Each endeavour as valid as the next. The integrity of any sense of values perverted by an overzealous egalitarianism. The bland would soon inherit the earth and although he knew he would not be there to see it, the thought still generated a crude TV-game-show kind of curiosity to amuse him in the quagmire. But this was no Florence, even if he was confined to bed again. This time, he was not in plaster. Nor in pain.

Left alone, the memories fading like the Caribbean lady's footsteps down the corridor of time, he longed for that containment to return. And still he could hear her laughter dancing over his doubts with verve. He needed pain.

# Cells

Life-defining,
life-confining
little bleeders.

They carry genes
And other hand-me-downs
in that fluid wardrobe of clutter
we call blood.

(I have always found
that the furniture of any given life
is minimalist by nature.)

Cells surround us,
pump within us.
They will always win.

Furniture survives
and mortals evaporate in a fusion of their own ephemera.

(That Sunday morning stroll through the Antiques Fair
should not induce a pre-roast glow of comfort,
but an eerie shudder from eternity.
That bric-a-brac from ages past
like discarded old coats hanging on hallstands
only mock our own mortality.)

A coffin brings the concept of a confining chamber
to perfection.
Everyone's agreed on that one.
Coffins are the ultimate cells.

Compact and utilitarian,
they are life-defining,
life-confining
little bleeders.

Don't knock them.
No one ever answers
and they will always win.

*

Pain had no concept of chronology, he realised. It was by nature arbitrary. And yet, little voices within him begged to differ, knowing how deliberate its application could be.

*I am on a tricycle rolling backwards down a steep garden path. These little legs I'm looking down on cannot compete with gravity. Behind me is an unseen garden gate. Within seconds, my complacency is in tears on the concrete. My skin is torn. My pride is shattered. My paradise is bruised.*

*Fear and blood are harbingers of new realities. This is my 'big bang'. My own. My very own. This is no theory. Pain finally makes me alive at this moment in time. The search has started. It is the start of everything. Memory is born.*

*I'm fairly certain that this first brush with death is where life began for me. The annals of human suffering must be enormous – too big for anyone to contemplate and, therefore, to care. So I accept that it's not important for it to be recorded that this is my first moment of remembered fright... indeed, my very first moment of remembrance. But the fact remains that this is a biggy; my first memory.*

*It's a wake-up call in the hotel of life. And I discover that my room is a torture chamber, only slightly tempered by my mother's love. Rushing through the back door, she brings her kitchen smells with her and kisses away the drama with her reassuring warmth.*

*Such details are pearls of comfort to adorn a scene of passion. But then again, pain itself is a poisoned string of pearls around the neck of masochism. I've never worn one, but feel sure I have one hidden somewhere in a drawer.*

He had spent his life believing that when pain was muted, all other feelings failed to fulfil their true potential. If ecstasy needed agony to display its full glory, surely Death would need the full participation of all the senses to give the ultimate thrill of one's lifetime. It was, after all, mooted as the climax to end all climaxes. How could pain be denied its place?

*Manifestations of every dart and lash ever endured since, slide like a razored adder through my sub-conscience.*

*Mine was not an immaculate conception, I realise. Nor a virgin birth. My father would never have allowed my mother the indulgence of such a solitary pleasure.*

Years after the fall, long after his family had left that house where he was born, that garden and that gate were bulldozed for the building of a road. The toddler's trauma had long since been tarmacked over, making it impossible for the adult ever to step inside that childhood pain again.

There was no going back.

*

'"Italians in the rain." That's what we're meant to be, you know?' he said. 'The Welsh! "Italians in the rain!" It's what George Bernard Shaw called us.'

'Did he now?' exclaimed the Caribbean cleaning lady, discreetly discarding her duster by the tray of sprays and polishes she carried with her everywhere.

He was sitting in the easy chair over by the window. His view was of trees and distant traffic. The collision he had just witnessed had been enough to kick-start a flurry of excitement and she waltzed over to join him, pretending to be interested.

'Such cavalier driving!' he explained. 'Very Italian.'

'Ah, the driving!' She started to understand. 'Yes, I've heard they're pretty operatic once they get behind them steering wheels. But I've never been there myself.'

'I saw it happen. Over there. Just a moment ago.'

'Yes, so I understand.'

'And we're meant to be very similar to Italians...'

'Except we're in the rain,' she interjected. 'Yes, I understand.'

'Not that I've ever felt any great affinity with the rain myself,' he mused.

'Now I got to agree with you there, Mr Davies. You see, I told you we'd have things in common! Back home in Jamaica, the rain is very different...'

'Jamaica! Ah, that's where you're from. I've never been there. Should have gone.'

'You being so well-travelled and all, Mr Davies! Yes, you should have gone.'

'I should. I should.'

'It's warm and dances all around you, killing off the dust. That's Jamaican rain. Nothing like the misery that falls here in Wales.'

It had been the yellow car's fault. It had deliberately cut in front of the silver-grey one, failing to complete the manoeuvre in time. Hence the crash. He had at first been exhilarated by the bang and the sudden sound of angry horns; then disappointed by the sight of two drivers gesticulating rather feebly before getting down to the mundane business of exchanging insurance details.

Someone had died earlier in the day. Not out there on the highway, but in the room next door. Who it was he did not know, but there had definitely been a passing. So much was controllable here, but not the sobs of relatives. He'd heard the wailing as its perpetrator passed his door. Hurried feet and furtive whispers had concealed the setting in motion of the well-oiled routine for corpse disposal and room change.

'We're always very open about these things,' Cathy had assured him when he mentioned the commotion to her. 'We have what they call "an open policy". But we don't dwell on things.'

They'd missed the accident, he thought. Whoever they were. If only they could have held on for a few more hours! Surely there was always something worth hanging on for.

But maybe not for everyone, he remembered. Some chose to go. Some went to meet the tide. Or caught an early flight.

Tired of the banter with the cleaner, his mind amused itself by mulling over the many euphemisms for suicide. To avoided further eye contact, in the hope that she would take the hint and carry on with her work, he turned his head towards the treetops, staring. He longed to be attended by a Jamaican nun, looking down upon him, her dour medication administered with a sunny radiance that scattered all the shed skin of humanity in a cloud of sequined black.

He couldn't have what he wanted. Not always. No one could.

*How could I have mistaken dust for Death in this place? There is no such thing as a Nevada night. Not with this much neon all around.*

*The desert haze descends. Engulfs me in its glare. I vow to take the first flight out of here, as soon as the authorities let me leave.*

*He will come home later, all alone.*

*Who the hell goes to Las Vegas to kill themselves? Is this Death as a holiday destination? Ridiculous and glorious? A cathedral to precariousness? He took a gamble. And won for once. Even though the odds were stacked against him. I have always known he was an unpredictable misfit. For three long years, he's bored me silly with all he knows on molecular physics. And now it turns out that he was just another academic who wanted to die in a playboy's town. Leaving me to face hotel security.*

*They charge for corpse storage. It's somewhere deep in the bowels of the hotel's basement, apparently. Where stiffs are kept cool. And someone has to pay. 'Refrigeration don't come cheap here, sir. Everybody needs it. It has a price.'*

*My immediate instinct is not to mourn but to turn to Mammon. Needs must! I check my credit cards. I check his insurance cover. For years to follow, the callousness I feel in these few days will greatly enhance my natural inclination to enjoy guilt.*

*This really is the final straw from him. His last elaborate farewell. There have been so many others throughout our stormy relationship. (There always are with the conversationally challenged! It's their only form of release.) So many ill-conceived dramas have been incompetently executed for my delectation by an emotional amateur. And even without an applause, he always came back centre stage for an encore.*

*Now at last, the sad, brainy bastard, has finally found the irony he always craved – as a slab of cold meat in arid air.*

*I understood him, but failed to see this final blow coming. Haunted by that discovery of him hanging there, I know I will not be able to forgive him for a long time. He has led me on too many dances; taken me on too many wild-goose chases and left me hanging for too long on those tenterhooks of dependency he'd cleverly created for me. How I've dangled like a rag doll for him! Holding on to that carousel of cruelty for grim death.*

*Except, of course, it was his grim death, after all. Not mine. He's the one left behind in Vegas when I take off. Does he know what irony means, I ask myself? Don't think he did. But maybe he does now.*

*Now the chips are down. I'm airborne. He is gone. With no dust to settle. In Vegas, dust is bleached into oblivion by the scorching sun. This I realise as the plane ascends and, flying home, I suddenly wake up to the fact that I will never see his face again. And cry.*

# Field

I had a field
and you built me a fence.

I sowed some grass
and you made me graze.

Containment is contentment for the chewing classes,
each munch a moment of
quivering concentration.

Free as fodder,
face firmly pointing downwards,
I ruminate over these eternal truths –
fields are liberating
fields confine.

The hedges that you planted are the edges of my world.
Green and thick and lush in their entrapment,
they are not so much a part of my life
as all around it.

You defined the limits.

You sussed the lay of the land
and fused the dimensions of the given turf
with my needs.

You made my desert meaningful
and gave me back that which was mine.

You gave meaning to monotony
and made me oh so grateful...
for a gate.

*

'Should I say it's alright for her to come?' he asked the other man. He felt that having to consult him of all people was a measure of his desperation, but knew he had no one else in whom to confide. 'What would you do?'

'Personally, if I don't see my ex-wife ever again, it will be too soon,' he responded. It was a measured, softly-spoken response, the poet noted. 'But that's me. We all must speak from our own experience.'

'Cathy said it was entirely up to me as well.'

'Well, there we are then! All I would add is that she deserves some brownie point for writing to you to ask in the first place. We have ex-spouses turn up here regularly to gloat. Others too, sometimes. Old scores to settle. Feuds in which they intend to have the last word. We're taught how to deal with it, of course. How to neutralise any potential conflict. But sometimes you just can't avoid a scene. It's most distressing when a so-called "visitor" turns up intent on causing one. But it happens.'

'"Shit happens" is the modern phrase you're looking for, I think,' chipped in the poet with a chuckle. 'Good old human nature never lets one down.'

'This Morwenna of yours sounds more sensitive to decorum than most.'

'Oh she's no Morwenna of mine!' came the response. 'Never was really. A youthful sham...'

'Best not to dwell on it, there's a good man,' the carer interrupted, handing back the letter.

It was taken by the old man's wizen hand and shakily returned to its envelope. His eyes remained fixed on the other man as he did so. He was making up the bed.

'Are you married now?' he asked, curiosity getting the better of him as he veered towards a reassessment of this usually rather distant carer.

'No,' answered the ex-soldier. 'What I have now is a partner.'

'Ah yes,' he responded with amusement. 'That's what everyone seems to have these days. Sounds much more multi-purpose and functional. Like these duvets we now all sleep under.'

The carer stood fully upright from his task of folding the bottom sheet around the mattress corner and, responding to the other man's amusement with a broad smile, said, 'I can still see the poet in you shining through there, my man. You have a way with words.'

Sitting in his armchair by the window, the frail man felt a sudden stirring in his prick, which shocked him greatly. The letter was shuffled from hand to hand in his lap and he tugged at the edges of his dressing gown as though he were in danger of betraying himself. But the rush was brief and over in a moment.

It was the unexpectedness of it which had shocked him. The

sudden display of kindness perceivable in those smiling eyes. The upright stance. The almost blatant potency of the man All these had conspired to evoke a rare response.

Caught unaware, he knew that surge of blood to be as cruel as it had been welcome. He felt sad again in an instance, not knowing what to do.

*Pretty churches have a lot more to answer for than the mediocre or mundane ones. They sanction far more folly.*

*An October afternoon in Nevern. How long ago! My brain blushes with the memory of such feigned innocence. The image fades and the sepia turns to crimson with embarrassment.*

*There are few signs of sudden sexual surges today. None in fact.*

*I give you the bride and groom. This man and wife – of sorts!*

*During all the preparations for these nuptials, no one seems to ask how sensible it is for us two to undertake this holy sacrament within these walls. I'm gay. She's neurotic. We're both immature. And all this is known to both parties. But sod all that. We crave normality. Or think we do. It turns out that that too is really an irrelevance to both of us. All is illusion. Then. And now.*

*I marry Morwenna because she's musical and find that thought rather wholesome. She marries me because she thinks she can mould me into a poet of sorts. So here we are, altar-bound. Two self-deluding wankers walking up the aisle, embarking on a doomed union, with bells above, ringing out their ridicule.*

*At the reception, I see even so-called friends sniggering behind privets, toasting two innocent tossers in champagne.*

*We never harmonise. Nothing ever rhymes.*

*After we part, she never hits the high notes of her supposedly glittering career. For my part, a few worthless words of regret are dribbled into the literary equivalent of a condom. And that is it. Diary kept. Disaster total. Divorce absolute.*

*A madrigal choir, with whom Morwenna has occasionally dabbled, sings during the service and afterwards, everyone says how like heaven they sounded. Her sister also sings. It's a folk song, in Welsh, which sounds wistful and wise and drains my mind of all sense of foreboding. Even here, on this day, I predict to myself that it's the only part of the proceedings I will remember with any clarity. (Omens are often more memorable than the catastrophes they precede.)*

'You need to consider her feelings in this,' the carer continued when he finally sat down beside the dying man at the corner of the freshly made-up bed. (It wasn't a hospital bed. The poet wasn't a patient. This was now his home and officially he had always to be referred to as a resident.)

Still trying to recall that song, he re-focussed on the man. He thought he was known as Bob, but could not be sure. One thing he did know with certainty was that he had a tattoo on his upper arm. He'd seen it a few days earlier in the hydro-therapy pool.

'Must I?' he asked in a mystified manner.

'She has done you the courtesy of asking you whether you would permit her to come visit you. That's all I'm saying. You must think beyond the present and consider her feelings when you are no longer here.'

'I've had nothing to do with her for nearly forty years. Barely knew anything about her bearings until I saw the address at the top of this letter. Never realised she lived so close.'

*Do I go back to Nevern now? No, never. The bleeding yew,*
*for which the churchyard is famous, no doubt still attracts*
*the curious and the mawkish; its crimson sap snapped up in*
*abundance by ever more sophisticated cameras. Holiday*
*mementos from a pretty spot. Remote. And wild. And riddled*
*with remorse.*

'She probably needs closure all the same,' insisted the man.

'Closure?' he echoed. 'Like a gate, you mean?'

'More like a full stop, mate.'

*Ding-dong! Here the lesson endeth. The classroom is dismissed.*

*I must remember what I said about churches and avoid them*
*like the plague. Until my death.*

## Score Sheet

Preserved on parchment –
the banal drivel of a jolly jingle
or the soul-enhancing ecstasy
of the simply divine?

You can never tell!

Listen to me now!
The untrained eye will never know
that which is echoed in the untrained ear.

Give me your finger.
Let me guide you

quivering over quavers,
quietly working our gymnastics on these dangerous bars.

Requiem
or commercial tune for selling chocolate?
It's all the same between the lines.
These hieroglyphics that I lead you over
will be forever howling or hallowed
in the hollow
where phlegm and fire burn within the soul.

It's the lump in the throat, you see.
The whistled fade-out of a life.

For us that is.

Parchments remain unemotional
And have never known the need to compose themselves.

Us mere mortals have always done it for them.

\*

Unlike most of his former lovers, he could physically recall
Pastor Oslo with vivid candour. He was nothing like the
stocky, thick-necked carer whose name he thought was Bob.
Pondering the point as he tried to make himself comfortable
in his newly-made bed, he realised that Pastor Oslo was
unlike most of the men with whom he'd sexually connected

throughout his life. And he could not recall where the Pastor Oslo name came from. Nicknames held no mystique for him. Their use always seemed to signify a mateyness and desire to create a clique to which he had never been able to relate; not since the alienating effect the use of nicknames had had on him during his childhood days.

Pastor Oslo was his one exception. And it was the contours of fine chiselled features that he remembered so well. That and the shadows created by sunlight through a window on his salty flesh.

His warmth in times of togetherness had been that generated by a cold climate. Nurtured by necessity. A frosty reproach inherent in his embraces. How he'd touched him for a while and tied him to his fate.

Words had been their original ties – fine, well-constructed words, handwritten to tie knots of mutual admiration and desire. The concept of a pen-pal was such a quaint one now. He stirred in anguish at the thought of the verbal impotence which was his latest affliction. How Pastor Oslo would have loved to see him suffering such a frustration!

Gradually, he had evolved into an e-mail buddy, the last messages exchanged some months earlier. No word had been spoken of the poet's imminent demise. They had not played any active part in each other's lives for over twenty years. Only at a distance. There was nothing he could do, either physically or spiritually. He had no need to know.

*It is the summer my pupils do even worse than usual in their exams and my mother dies. I am in the mood to accept chastisement with a suitably enthusiastic ardour.*

*Fair and pale and almost devoid of any demonstrative*

*displays of emotion, he's a Lutheran minister and will teach me
everything I know about bondage. From initiation to fulfilment,
I am his in every possible meaning of that word at this time.*

*Thirty years and more have passed and still his passion
lingers on within me; the kindest friend I ever had. This I tell
everyone who cares to listen. Him, I never told. Others in my
life have been more generous and resilient, but none was ever
kinder.*

*Why did you take so long to deliver this one, big bad dog?*

*Castles intrigue him and, therefore, like the nerve endings of
my entire body, Wales is one big playground for him all this
summer long. I spend his frequent visits to see me ferrying him
from fortress to fortress. I am incapable of insurrection and
totally besotted by his immobilising skills. For him, castles are
naturally synonymous with conquest and being a natural
dominator, his affinities are always with the oppressor. I yield to
his occupation in euphoria.*

*He always insists on eating well, as well, can become almost
visibly intoxicated by the smell of forests and loves the fibrous
friction of rope on skin. These are the memories of him I know
will last. Through knowing him I grow a quiet realisation that
men whose calling is predominantly spiritual or cerebral are
often blessed with a keener, honed adherence to the senses than
manual workers. The farmer, the garage mechanic and the
abattoir worker, say, live and work with an all-prevailing
assault on their sensory organs every day, and thus, become
immune to such exquisitely simple sensations. The poet and the
pastor, on the other hand, inhabit a different realm, consume a
different diet. Words, not nerve-endings, are what bring raw
experiences into their worlds.*

A crisis in the night brought the agency nurse to his attendance. He was hanging halfway out of the bed, the tubes jarring, the pain visible in his torrential sweat.

'Don't you worry now, my friend. We'll soon get you comfortable again.'

For a while, the poet was delirious. Clutching those postcards from his past, he knew they often lied but still manage to tell it entirely as it was. He held on to a child-like faith in an absolute truth.

The American-trained, Filipino-born carer had never heard the word Morwenna before. She wondered what this thing was. A man or beast? She had heard of Oslo, however. But had no idea where it was on a map.

It never occurred to her as she moved swiftly to get this sick man under her care through the night that they might be a former wife and lover, respectively.

*He's still there, of course. If not in Oslo, somewhere else. Still leading people to the Cross. Still tending to their needs. His is a resolute life; focused and astonishingly open if all he's ever told me is to be believed. Despite all the evidence to the contrary, his flock, it seems, simply refuses to believe him capable of such unorthodox idiosyncrasies. Or perhaps they believe what they see well enough, but chose to accept him as a flawed instrument, setting their sights beyond the peculiarities of the man and concentrating instead on the salvation he represents with such conviction. I often wondered how it was. And when, way back then, I'd ask him about this out loud, he'd smile one of his mischievous smiles – a mixture of malevolence and grace – saying only that Norway was big enough for many men.*

Pastor Oslo always made his native land seem so cold and clean and nondescript, the poet always thought of it as a clean page. A moral void. A treat for lungs.

Lying there, once that bewildered, exotic stranger had subdued the agitation, he felt a heroic admiration for brave breaths drawn on the fringes of the world. So solitary and forlorn, he cherished the memory of that Nordic peace he had never actually known and, once left alone again, wept for that long-lost imagined idyll.

*

'At least you're not in any pain,' said Morwenna, leaning forward in her chair when the conversation reached a lull.

'That's true,' he agreed, his feeble voice masking the wry derision he felt inside.

'It's very good of them to set aside a corner of the lounge for us like this,' she added, lifting up her cup of tea and saucer in a gesture of gratitude.

'Not really,' he disagreed without acrimony. 'I don't think it's ever used much. We're all too ill for idle gossip and macramé sessions. And we all have a television set in our rooms.'

'Yes, I suppose one has to provide that sort of thing these days.'

'Don't know why they bother. All they seem to have on during the day are programmes about people who are about to move homes, antiques and a thing called *Countdown*. It doesn't auger well for happy viewing for the dying.'

'Good to see you haven't lost your sense of humour, at least,' said Morwenna.

'I've lost plenty else,' he retorted. 'And so have you. Whatever happened to your Titian hair?'

'It turned into a Kyffin Williams,' she jokingly replied. 'Black and white sheep dogs now roam my scalp in wild abandon.'

As she'd spoken, she'd combed her free hand through the hair and his eyes had followed suit. The demure, determined girl of his youth had turned into an ageing hippy.

He had almost failed to recognise her when she was first shown in some minutes earlier. Making the effort to get to his feet, he'd struggled to make the drip-stand and piss-bag as inconspicuous as possible. They'd exchanged an awkward kiss. More of an allusion to a kiss than a kiss itself. That old woman's hair had momentarily brushed against his hollow cheek.

She was also fatter than he had expected. A comfortable-looking jumper hung around her frame. Not unkempt exactly. But careless.

'I'm glad you seem to have had a successful life, all in all,' she ventured. 'Apart from that awkward business at the school, of course. An unfortunate end to a teaching career.'

'Oh you saw all that, did you?'

'I'm afraid so. My mother sent me the cuttings.'

'And did you follow my success as well?'

'Not really. People mentioned you sometimes. I've seen a few of your volumes in various bookshops. They always struck me as being rather thin. That's probably been the way with modern poetry. I haven't really kept up with things.'

'You used to take an interest.'

'Times change,' she answered.

'And you are no longer with Richard, I understand.'

'Good heavens no. Not for years. Moved on.'

'Sorry to hear that,' he said with sincerity.

'Kate came from that marriage. So that was OK.'

'You should have had others.'

'Children or marriages?' she asked cynically.

'I meant children,' he replied.

'No, any more would have stifled my career. One was just enough.'

'Oh yes, of course,' he conceded, pretending to be in sympathy with her concept of a career.

Before taking her leave, she asked him if he'd like her to bring some pot with her next time.

He responded with an incredulous, 'What?'

'I could easily get hold of some if you fancied a spliff,' she replied.

'I shouldn't think they'd allow illegal substances in here,' he said rather priggishly.

'Oh honestly! I would have thought this was the last place where the terms "allowed" and "not allowed" were given very high priority. What does any of that matter by the time you reach here? You were always such a damn puritan.'

'She didn't use to be so bohemian,' is all he had to tell Cathy of the visitation later.

'I'll pretend you haven't told me about the cannabis,' was her matter of fact response. 'It is true that we see all sorts of things go on in here. All we ask is that everyone respects the integrity of the other residents.'

So, Morwenna was right. What a depressing thought. But a puritan, indeed? How dare she? A failed masochist, maybe. That would be nearer the mark, he judged. He'd loved the lifestyle; but couldn't stand the pain! Like the wannabee surgeon who couldn't stand the sight of blood. Denied pain as he was, life was being reduced to a series of cheap jibes. It really was that absurd. Except of course that a horror of the tactile is so much more repulsive than a horror of the visual. His brief marriage to Morwenna had taught him that. What you feel always being more vivid than what you see. Or so he had always convinced himself.

Had he always been so seemingly self-assured? And therefore so self-opinionated in the eyes of the world? Had his posturing always stopped him from being truly popular? As a poet? As a man?

The poems, at their best, were characterised by a crystal clear use of words, he'd always thought, while the attempts at prose had always, rightly, been condemned as pretentiously verbose. And he was constantly analytical. Even now. Obsessively delving. Days away from Death, perhaps. Dissecting at a distance. In work as in life itself. A cold, self-conscious fish.

He had been told by a master sadist not to allow his pain to be contaminated by his conscience. Those very words had been used: 'Let go, boy! Give in to it. Don't contaminate the purity of the pain I'm giving you by your pansy conscience.' Or words to that effect. Similar words. Synonyms. Who could be precise with remembered pain? The mechanics of the brain were set so as to automatically distort, diminish or destroy pain. It had to do with preserving sanity and propagating life. Ask any mother? She knows about pain and its inherent amnesia.

But the suppression of the excruciating also had a major downside for mankind – it made us immune from the inability to inflict it on others. Good old brain! A metropolis of infinite sophistication. The sewage system being worthy of extra special mention. Since memories were flushed away in an instance, we could do unto others as someone else once did unto us. With scant concern.

*'Inhale the pain. Exhale the guilt.' A cold, dark glove hovers over my cheek as he speaks; almost caressing, never connecting with my skin; threatening an act of kindness but never quite committing. This is a comfort zones – one of those sanctioned lulls of rest a tormentor allows his victim. It is where pain is reflective and the smell of leather is at its most pungent.*

*Angels hover in the distance, threatening the two-winged comfort of vengeance and redemption. A constant sense of darkness masks their voyeuristic glee. They only watch and never intervene, waxing lyrically on the edges of salvation and sex.*

*The greased-up forearm strives to sustain my subservience and the tears that fall from my eyes bear witness to the heart-beats which he always claims to feel inside me.*

*How these images linger on the corners of the backstreets of this half-forgotten folly! Dysfunctional lamp-posts perversely shedding their weary light upon the mayhem – adding to the menace, rather than offering illumination.*

*I stubbornly maintain my right to seek some higher goal. Some semblance of a spiritual dimension. Aimless. Blind as a bat. The elegance with which I suffer belying the futility of my search. He, for his part, always tells me I am mad. That a comic book salvation is the most I can achieve. And even that is only possible by total capitulation to his creed.*

*He leads me to the belfry. Leaves me to swoop through the chiaroscuro air; good chasing evil chasing good chasing evil in a*

*game of two colours – both black. As a failed fantasist, it is*
*fitting that I hide my pain in the unrelenting shades of night.*
  *My ordeal is silent.*
  *My spirit triumphant.*
  *I pretend to be free.*

## Stamp

Rectangular, self-adhesive little beauty.
Not quite a symbol of possession,
but proof of passage.

Peculiarly perforated
and cruel in its simplicity
yours
is rare enough to be collectable.

As a verb,
You're the mail that puts its foot down;
as a noun,
you seal my fate.

Returned to sender,
I'm delivered back into your hands
for ripping open and rereading.

(You dropped me in the post box;
you waited for the postman's knock.)

Consume that which you have written.
Let your eyes lust for each letter
and when you finally finish with me
I shall await the final crush within your fist –
ready for the fire.

Your thumb,
so firm and subtle in the pressing,
was all it took each time
to make that imprint stick
and shape the top right-hand corner of my soul.

I am destined to forever feel
your image
still branded on my skin
like pain in transit –
postage paid, of course.

(There's now no need to lick, you know.
You save on spit – but personally, I miss the taste!)

\*

'Was it all spit and polish then? Frogmarching across the
Brecon Beacons for queen and country?' teased the poet from
his prostrate position flat on his back in bed.

'Not quite, old man. A few more late starts and longer pub
stops than the army would allow,' Bob jovially replied.

'I can see it did you good.'

135

'Well! I miss the camaraderie, I suppose. And all that walking did me good.'

They were relaxed in each other's company in a way which would have seemed impossible six weeks earlier, when the poet took up residency. Mutual suspicion had given way to mutual respect. Necessity may well have been the main motivation on both their parts, but neither wanted to admit it.

'I've been a walker, you know? In my day.'

'Yes, I know. Wrote books and poems about your travels and all, did you not?'

'Oh no! I never saw poetry as a branch of tourism. That school of creativity has always been an anathema to me.'

'Sorry, my friend. I've never really been much of a reader, if truth be known.'

'Don't worry, I was never much of a walker. Although I did once spent a whole week walking through Eifionydd and Snowdonia. I was what you might call "under orders". Showing off the beauties of north Wales to a Norwegian friend.'

'That parson guy? You mentioned him before.'

'He thought us Welsh were too easy for oppressors. Always squabbling amongst ourselves.'

'I've never felt very Welsh,' confided Bob.

'Well! That's probably very wise if you don't want a lot of angst cluttering up your life,' replied the poet.

For most of his creative life he'd felt neglected on the Welsh literary scene; an outsider despite it all. Had it not been for a favourable review here and a minor prize there, thrown at him from over the English border, he feared the Welsh literati would happily have continued to ignore him all his life.

*It's only when the Welsh establishment felt shamed into it*

*that they finally and begrudgingly decided to embrace me,' I tell
the pastor.*

*Pastor Oslo replies by telling me I do not deserve to be
embraced by anyone – at least not in the way I crave.*

'It's only when the establishment really felt it couldn't
ignore me any longer that they begrudgingly decided to
embrace me,' he said to Bob.

Bob made no reply.

One day in a Cardiff office, he continued to them both – and
it was always Cardiff, no matter to whom he told the story or
how many years had elapsed between each telling – someone
conceded that he had, after all, to be made 'one of us'. 'Us' –
in this instance – being that familial, tribal, fake sense of
fraternity which is fine for administrative purposes and
fostering a sense of identity, but which did not always lay
easy with the creative spirit.

It was true that his work had been all symmetry and form
and rarely shared that angst of belonging which seemed to so
dominate the literary landscape of the twentieth century in
Wales.

He remembered walking with Pastor Oslo, talking as he
did so of his efforts to learn Welsh. To have failed was both
alienating and consoling, he had claimed, but his companion
had continuously dragged it back to Norway at every turn.
Norwegians, he had insisted, also experienced a similar
dichotomy of belonging. It had something to do with the past,
he said.

Had they not already been to both Cricieth Castle and the
Lloyd George Museum in Llanystumdwy that very day? Did
the present not confront its past at every corner? Would
certain European nations' psychological well-being not be

better served by refraining from such an indulgence? These were the questions asked, the proposals put forward. These very words were spoken. Or words to that effect.... Always words to that effect.

*As we ramble, both verbally and on foot, I long for the perfect tearoom, where a buxom Welsh woman serves scones still fresh from her caresses and warmed by her smile; with salted butter, strawberry jam that is, if not home-made, then at least bought at the local WI bring-and-buy; and tea that poured from a blue and white teapot into matching cups.*

*It is a retreat to motherly things. An abdication of responsibility.*

Revisiting the museum, twelve months earlier, his thoughts were only of himself. He was there alone and arrived by car. No longer was he troubled by a myriad interpretations of nationality. He now knew himself that much better and saw himself as nothing more than a minor poet, grey and spent, paying homage to the most colourful statesmen of his day. They were both day-trippers to fame, Lloyd George and he, albeit at different ends of the celebrity scale.

*My poetry is unfashionable now. Unloved. And, worse of all, unread. What fame I had has passed. Everything is past. And as I sip some hideous concoction from a waxy cardboard cup this chill May morning beside the Dwyfor, it dawns on me that my lack of fulfilment has cannibalised what little soul I ever had. And that failure is the greatest pain of all.*

Artefacts from his life will never be neatly laid-out for public perusal. His grave will never be a shrine by clear water.

Three days after his return from that second visit to Llanystumdwy, he was given his prognosis.

A few days before the end of his confinement, a genuine card arrived. It was brought to his room by Cathy, who found herself having to rip open the envelope on his behalf.

'It's a little bit stiff, isn't it? Shall I do it?'

Those hands would never hold a reefer now. Let alone a pen.

It was from someone called Jeff, whom he could barely remember as an acquaintance from some dubious aspect of his life.

'That was nice of him, wasn't it?' Cathy continued the pretence of normality. 'Shall we leave it here?'

The obligatory bowl of grapes was at last accompanied by a greeting card.

He turned his head on the pillow, his hollow eyes scrutinising the display. It was a sunny day he saw. A gentle breeze he felt upon his skin. His senses were gathering a renewed vividness as his outward countenance descended into hazy chaos. Inside, his heart was dancing with his youth, the rhythm of a golden oldie as clear as a bell.

*Midges. Flies. And then, bees. Lots of bees. Stinging. Raging. Rampaging through our picnic. Is this just the death of a summer's day? Or the death of my faith in summer days?*

*Wine spills over the edges of cheap glasses. Mini-screams of anger stain the masculine veneer of our idyll. Men who rarely swear, curse profusely. Questions carefully avoided over many months of bonding are asked out loud.*

*It is man-made. This tiny St Cwyfan's Church-in-the-sea, off* the coast of Anglesey. All churches are, of course. They serve a man-made need. Picturesquely perched on an oval erection out at sea, it is but a stone's throw from the site of Prince Llywelyn's court at Aberffraw. The two landmarks are divided only by traces of sand-dunes and in-breeding.

Brian hits his head on the gravestone he has been leaning on for support as the swarming blitz begins. Is he the first to swear? To ask if bees live out at sea?

People are buried all around us. As an unkempt cemetery skirts the ramshackled church, the tide isolates the dead here. Treacherous tiny steps give access. The worshippers stopped climbing long ago.

No one mourns here now. Except we did, that day.

We had climbed with care and sat around our Enid Blyton-like discovery. A Famous Five of 1960s youth – radical, didactic and as abandoned as the church itself. We put the world to rights, some of us flirting discreetly in the haze. We had found our own little secret for the afternoon. Grown-up boys. Not yet men – not really! All gay – although we have not all realised that truth at this stage and none of us knows the term, because it has not yet been invented. Words are yet to be corrupted. Enlightenment is gradual.

Strange, though, how we have all gravitated towards each other at university, doing so in genuine innocence it seems to me, even in retrospect. At this moment in time there is no obvious common thread between us, but unbeknown to any of us, some of the assembled are destined to hate each other with time.

Before the invasion, others occasionally venture over to the island from the beach. Just a few. Small groups intent on snapping up the photo opportunity, tut-tutting the fact that the church's dignity has long since been corroded by salty sea breezes and seagull shit.

The bell is missing from its designated spot. So no souls are ever summoned here. All who visit come voluntarily.

Wine guzzles onto grass as the spitfires continue their menace. And Dafydd tells everyone to be calm. An Anglesey native, he assumes some acquaintance with these invaders and tries to mediate.

Will favours retreating to the mainland forthwith, whilst Dermot analyses the chances of further attacks upon our persons. After the initial swoop, he thinks this unlikely, on condition that we abandoned the provisions we'd brought with us. (Students go for picnics in these far-off days. It is a bygone age of prudence. Now, they go for 'piss-ups', and other even more crudely-named excesses, in places further flung than churches out at sea.)

Forced to our feet, we hover near the edge. The sea lays several hundred feet below. No fence or wall peripherates the site and it is no place for the inebriated.

Will, the strongest of us and the one we all secretly adore, dances perilously close to the drop.

Dafydd and Dermot both talk their way through our predicament; Dafydd taking stock – no one has actually been stung, he notes, and this I remember as being pivotal to his reasoning – and Dermot resorting to science. Both are destined to aspire to be leaders in their later lives, in various fields. And neither will succeed.

Brian, shirtless on the ground, rolls around on the grass following his highly-dramatised concussion, claiming immunity. As the edge gets closer, he stops and wipes the long hair from his face; his instinct for survival still intact, for now.

*We do the inevitable. And what a sorry sight we must seem to those sunning themselves on the beach. Five scruffy students stepping down from a derelict edifice. No longer cavalier in our camaraderie. Our various ways of changing the world abandoned, shoo-ed off by a freak of nature.*

*Having packed what we managed to retrieve of our food into the boot, we cram into Dafydd's Ford Prefect and drive away.*

*One of us was destined to die in Las Vegas. The rest of us, as far as I know, are still alive... for now.*

## Bells

Where no bell tolls,
no one's sleep is shattered by a gong,
no class is ever summoned or dismissed,
no feast consumed,
no marriage marked by chimes.

Where no bell tolls,
the dead remain unburied.

And as for me, I'm lucky.

The bell without a clanger
In the belfry in my brain
displays its Man of Letters badge with pride
and makes its muted din
inordinately soft
in various vacant parishes

along the pilgrim's trail.

Unfed, unwed
and thick as two short planks

– forgive me my forthrightness,
but vacancies offer no comfort
to those in search of intellectual finesse –

at least I'm still alive,

awake,
aware of what you're doing

and unfettered
by the ding-dong discipline
of your vast domain.

*

It came from the sea. Of that much he was sure. That swarm
of bees. That wave of youthful chums. That mist of deepening
delirium.

The delivered memories became more sun-drenched with
each passing day. The harsh hues were dazzled out of existence
as the end approached.

The black face of the Caribbean cleaning lady hovered over
his, wondering whether she should seek assistance, not sure if
he was dead or not.

As he coughed a breath, she startled backwards in relief and told him that she had been threatened with dismissal for spending too much time talking to the residents.

'"Fraternising" they called it,' she insisted. 'Overfamiliarity with the residents. Me? Huh!'

Outraged by the suggestion, the poet rallied to her defence. What prigs these people were! As he himself had been for much of his life, he thought, shaming himself with the memory of always refusing to send his mother a postcard from his many travels. 'My poems are my postcards. You don't need anything else,' he used to tell her. What a sanctimonious shit she'd had for a son!

'You keep me sane in here,' he told the talker. 'I rather like our little chats.' Before disappearing again, he assured her that he would do everything in his power to help her keep her job, 'Even if it's the last thing I do.'

The significance of such a promise was not lost on her and she soon shut up, retreating to her chores in embarrassment.

*At last, the dog is here.*

*I do not know where it came from but it lands on my face like a shabby mop. Wet and panting. In truth it has come from the sea, of course. That much is obvious. It is always the sea. All my land-locked life I have been surrounded by it and not realised its power is relative to the moon.*

*Today, I am confronted by the sea. I am young again. Sunbathing on a foreign beach, surrounded by beautiful people whose bronzed bodies they believe to be adornments to the golden sand, I am assaulted by my damp deliverer.*

*The shudder and the scream coincide. As does the dog's retreat. Flung in the air by my instantaneously upright jolt, it*

*barks in indignation and rolls over in the sand before shaking its*
*salty fur and leaping away from the laughter, back towards the*
*sea.*

*He does not seem to have either a master or mistress. No one*
*takes charge.*

*The sun steals my senses for a moment. My face smells of old*
*dog. My sensibilities tell me that my main concern should not*
*be the dog but my dignity. I am suddenly the centre of attention.*
*Some smile in sympathy, feeling my embarrassment. Others*
*laugh openly, glad of the comic relief which has distracted them*
*from their own narcissism.*

Those who laughed at him were mostly bronzed queens. Since
he had never felt anything other than contempt for that
precious and pointless brigade of misfits, it was easy for him
to dismiss their unkindness at this time.

Even in primary school, he had never been drawn to the
petulant and pretentious. His natural inclination had always
been towards the rough boys – the truants, the rugby players
and the ne'er-do-wells. In reality, they rarely let him into their
world. But still he hovered on the edges.

Some boys straddled both worlds, it was true to say, and
those he envied most of all. Because they belonged essentially
to the thigh and fist brigade, they were never picked on or
ostracised for being brainy, as he had been. His own kind
proved to be few and far between, and except when pertinent
to do so, were mostly to be avoided. The boys he aspired to
be with were the ones who scrambled towards adulthood with
brawn and cheek.

Suddenly, Billy Collins stood tall again. He had been his
very best pre-pubescent friend. And he was there now, captured

on the picture side of the postcard – a crystal-clear presence on the beach. Blessed with a mop of thick, jet-black hair and a gangster's gait, he had loved to play football but had also indulged the poet's childhood passion for little plays and dramatic monologues with equal enthusiasm.

Scrawny and scruffy, he would sometimes disappear with the gang for hours on end, only to return and tantalise him with hints of the mischief they'd been up to. Although always sworn to deadly secrecy before any furtive detail could fall from Billy's lips, he always felt privileged. It was Billy Collins who allowed him a glimpse of that other sinister world, away from piano lessons and lavish Sunday teas, he so longed to be a part of.

His mother always said that Billy's mother was too inept to cope with rationing. Hence his rake physique and shabby clothes. Lying there dying, he could hear her voice condemning. It rang out across the beach, drowning the pain of derision.

Curiously, she had liked Billy Collins. Looking back, he realised how rare that was. She'd encourage him to stay and watch the better TV programmes with him and often fed him generously. But not his dog. Never the dog. The mongrel always had to remain outdoors, tied up by the back door.

After the eleven-plus, which our poet passed and Billy failed, they rarely saw each other. Their childhood crumbled. Their old school was demolished. They never ever strolled along a beach together.

*That evening, in a bar, this Australian guy who's built like a rugby player and has American-style teeth, dazzling white and plentiful, commiserates with me. He tells me that he saw exactly what happened. And he doesn't know where that god-darn dog came from either. Made a beeline for my face, though, he says. And wasn't that something?*

*I don't take it to be a chat-up line at the time. I'm too busy trying to forget that dog. But the following day, he and I are both back on the beach, sharing a tube of Factor 15 and a double towel. There isn't a dog in sight. No Mother. And no Billy.*

\*

Billy's hand was beneath the sheet resting on top of his.

No, it was Bob's hand resting on his own beneath the sheet.

'It's only me,' the carer seemed compelled to say as the dying man awoke with a startled jolt. The hand was duly removed.

He looked toward the carer, disappointed by the disappearance of his touch. This man called Bob – he searched his face for eyes. But eye contact was beyond what Bob could cope with at a time of great intensity. Instead, he had fixed his gaze on the treetops visible through the window.

*A small boy takes a bucket to his Gran and says, 'Go on, kick this. My dad says I'll get a bike when you do!'*

*This is my final punch-line. Is it time to go? A time to go....*

*When he told me it was time to go, it was raining cats and dogs outside. Now that I do remember. He said it with an impotent benevolence: that is to say, in a calm and comforting voice that still offered no way out. A scandal could still be averted if I went, he said. So go I must.*

*And go I must....*

*I get soaked running for the bus.*

*His name is Jenkins and his face still shines with a peculiarly*

*paternal indignation inside my head. 'The good of the school...*
*and all that.' A mantra for educationalists everywhere. My own*
*good name and all, he insisted... best for everyone concerned.*
*That sort of thing. So much of 'that sort of thing' has bogged me*
*down, I cannot recall it all. Can life really be like a* Carry On
*film with poetry prizes thrown in for good measure? Oh,*
*Matron! Is it really time to go?*

He was thirty-seven when he visited the Bamford Comic
Collection at Holmfirth. It had, no doubt, been something to
do on a wet afternoon in deepest, darkest Yorkshire. Museums
always are, all over the world. With whom he'd spent that day
had been obliterated from the memory. He was there alone
now. That is all that mattered.

*I am well and truly all alone now. That is all that matters.*

Classics of their type, those saucy icons of the grotesque
had once been posted with a cheeky grin by millions. Now,
they were collectables. Half-forgotten artefacts from spent
summers. Hideous in their innocence. Unlike their modern
equivalent (and the busty blondes that characterised most of
them) these old tokens of regard were never touched up or
computer-enhanced. What you saw is what you got in those
days. Comic candyfloss that failed to rot the moral fibre of a
long-forgotten seaside generation.

*In my seaside postcard museum, Death is a giant nun floating*
*on a velvet sea, hitting lighthouses that don't work, perched on*
*rocks that really hurt.*

*Dutifully stamped and sent, her image now descends into the*
*maelstrom of my mind. The bitch dutifully delivers door to door,*
*regardless of the weather.*

*Do you wish you were here? Don't be daft!*

# Duster

Yellow square
of clinging comfort
in my hand

gathers in its tidy grip
the shadowy remains
mysteriously discarded
over the surfaces
of my material pride and joy.

As I shake it
from an open window,

all the debris, dirt and dead skin
shed during the life I've lived
floats away,

looking back at me
as oblivion beckons,
foolishly thinking
that I'm only waving them a temporary
Goodbye.

*

On the day he died, the solution to 4-across in *The Times'* crossword was 'Twinge'. The solution to 1-down was 'Hilarity'. He experienced both at the point of passing and they crossed at the 'i'.

A few days later, his obituary in the same paper dismissed him as a, *'Welsh poet of minor interest who became fashionable in the early 1970s, but whose reputation waned with the emergence of a less anaemic, more politically-charged generation of poets from the principality.'*

The *Western Mail* took the opportunity of his death to mull once more over the 'aura of mystery' which hung over his sudden departure, twenty years earlier, from the minor public school where he'd taught. According to speculation, certain articles written by him had appeared in a 'specialist' magazine aimed at the sado-masochistic homosexual market and had caused an outcry amongst parents when a sixth-former had brought the publication to the attention of his parents. Others offered the theory that he was simply a crap teacher. Either way, he warranted no more than a few column inches and no picture.

Given the task of clearing his room, Bob found several hand-written poems amongst his things. Taking a snap decision and breaking all the rules, he folded them neatly and hid them away in his pocket. He wanted something of his own to remember him by and took a curious satisfaction from sensing that the dead man would approve.

## Acknowledgements

I am indebted to all those who provided specific information and general encouragement during the writing of these stories. The wise comments of friends such as Bil, Carol, Eurgain, Ioan and Luned were particularly appreciated.

I'm very grateful to Gwen Davies, not only for her enthusiasm, but also her perception, honesty, and constructive suggestions.

I thank lloyd robson and all at Parthian.

To Steve, for his constant support and much else besides, my special thanks.

Earlier versions of two of these stories ('Just Like My Jeff' and 'Sunset at Kastro's') appeared in *I Lawr Ymhlith y Werin* (Gomer Press, 2002).

Aled Islwyn